DISCARDED

DRED A TALE OF THE GREAT DISMAL SWAMP

DRED A TALE OF THE GREAT DISMAL SWAMP

H. J. Conway, Harriet Beecher Stowe

DRED A TALE OF THE GREAT DISMAL SWAMP

H. J. Conway, Harriet Beecher Stowe

ISBN : 4444000066172PB

Reprint 2016 in India by

Facsimile Publisher
12 Pragati Market
Ashok Vihar, Ph-2
Delhi-110052, India
E-mail: books@facsimilepublisher.com

DRED:

A TALE OF

THE GREAT DISMAL SWAMP.

A DRAMA, IN FOUR ACTS,

FOUNDED ON THE NOVEL OF THE SAME TITLE, BY
Mrs. H. B. STOWE.

DRAMATIZED BY

H. J. CONWAY, Esq.

New-York:
JOHN W. AMERMAN, PRINTER,
No. 60 WILLIAM-STREET.

DRED.

ACT I.

SCENE I.—*The Canema Plantation. The family mansion of the Gordons on the R. H., with veranda, and steps on the L. H.; mid-distance the negro quarters, and extreme distance cotton fields—the whole having the glow of southern scenery. Plantation negroes, male and female, in their best attire, discovered. Curtain rises to the symphony of the*

OPENING CHORUS.

"Welcome home to Miss Nina,
    De North Car'lina rose;
Miss Nina's like de rays ob de sun,
    She sheds light where ebber she goes;
        Welcome! Welcome!

" On Canema plantation
    We all is happy and gay,
Den welcome home to Miss Nina,
    Home. At home for ever to stay;
        Welcome! Welcome!
At home for ever to stay."

POMP, C., (*after chorus.*)

I declar I feels just de same as if Miss Nina was my young missus; all de same as yourn.

CUFF. (R.) So you orter; you is a Gordon nigger, too.

POMP. I is dat, honey. All you niggers b'longs to Miss Nina, and I b'long to her Uncle John.

CUFF. Uncle John Gordon! And he is a real Gordon, too.

POMP. Ebbery inch. Guess if you see him mad once, you'd clar yourself mighty quick.

CUFF. Yah! Yah! Yah! De Gordons am de debble when dem backs is up.

POMP. Lor' bress you, niggers, you'd orter seen de ole mas'r dis mornin' when he done got one of he fits. Dar he was, tearin' round, fit to split, stampin' up an' down, an' swearin' like mad. He done get our Jake tied up dar, before de house door, swearin' he gwoin to cut him in pieces; an' I must do it.

CUFF. But you didn't.

POMP. You shall hear. Ebbery one ob de niggers was a lookin' on, and dar was ole missus, too, up in de balcony. Ole mas'r he cry out, " I'll teach you; I won't bear it of you, you dog, you. I'll cut you up into inch pieces. You won't 'bey my orders. I'll kill you." Den de missus say, "No, you won't, and you know you won't, and *dern* too, know you won't. It will all end in smoke, as it always does !" (*All the negroes laugh.*) Golly ! you'd orter see de mas'r turn round on de missus. " Hold your tongue," he say, "I will be master in my own house. Infernal dog ! cut him up, Pomp ! give it him ! What are you waiting for !" Den I say, if mas'r pleases. Den he fly off agin—", If I please ? I do please; go at him; thrash away !— Stay ! I'll come down myself." Den he was comin' down de stairs .like mad, when he foot slip, an' he pitch head first right agin de post whar Jake was tied up. Den we pick him up, an' he say to Jake, " Dar, now, I hope you is satisfied; you have killed me. I shall be laid up for a mouth, and all for you, you ungrateful dog you! Den we brush de dust off his clothes—he go into de house—I untie Jake, and dar, sure enough, it did all end in smoke.

        (*All laugh. Whip heard to crack outside,* L. U. E.)

ALL. Here's Miss Nina ! Here's Miss Nina !

POMP. Den ebbery one of you mind what I tell you about de reception of her.

(TOM TIT *sings outside,* L. U. E, " Ole Virginny never tire !")

POMP. Now, niggers, fall into de line to reception Miss Nina.

        Enter TOM TIT, U. E. L. *dancing and singing.*

TOM TIT. " O, I is going to glory !" " Taint Miss Nina ; it's Mas'r Gordon.

ALL. (*In dismay.*) Mas'r Tom Gordon.

TOM TIT. Mas'r Tom ! No. You tink I come in singing if it am he—no—no—it is Uncle John Gordon—Hurrah ! Ole Virginny never tire.

ALL. Hurrah for Mas'r Gordon.

TOM TIT *goes up, and ushers in* UNCLE JOHN *and Mr.* JEKYL, L. H. *All the negroes crowd round* UNCLE JOHN.

UNCLE JOHN. Phew ! Stand out of my way ! Give me room to breathe ! Out of my way, I say !

TOM TIT. (*Waves them back.*) Niggers, I is really surprised at your want of breeding—stand back ! (*They all fall back.*) Mr. John Gordon—I hope you'll excuse dem—dey can't be all like me.

UNCLE JOHN. Well done, Tom Tit. But where is my niece, my darling Nina !

TOM TIT. She has not yet arrived, sir ; some of de common niggers is watching for her at de gate, and we are here to give a reception to oar young lady in a 'spectable manner becoming a Gordon: in de mean time would you gentlemen please to step in and partake of our hospitality. We are proud to welcome. (*Sings*)

        " A fine old Virginny gentleman,
          One of the olden time."

All the negroes chorus this. TOM TIT, *with great ceremony, leads the way up into the house, followed by* UNCLE JOHN, *laughing, and* Mr. JEKYL.

Bell rings inside the house.

POMP *to* CUFF. You hear dat!

CUFF. To be sure I does.

POMP. And what am it!

CUFF. It am a bell. *(Bell again, louder.)*

POMP. It am a bell, am it! and it am your ole missuses bell, Miss Nesbit's, and it am ringing for you.

CUFF. I ain't no bird. I can't be in dis yer place, receptioning young missus, and in dat yer place, 'tending on ole missus; and I ain't a going to, nuther.

Enter, during this, from house, AUNT MILLY, *with her bunch of housekeepers' keys at her girdle. She takes* CUFF *by the ear.*

CUFF. Oh! oh! Aunt Milly, I was comin' dis yer blessed minute— Oh! oh!

AUNT MILLY *leads him by the ear into the house. All laugh.*

POMP. Now, niggers, we'll precessionade down by the revenue of trees, and meet young missus come

MUSIC.—*Chorus repeated as they exeunt, as scene closes,* U. E. L. H.

SCENE II.—*An Apartment in the Canema Mansion.*

POMP. (*Peeps in,* L. H. L. E., *and enters.*) I is stole in at de back do', as I know mas'r will want me for some ting or anodder, besides dis chile wants a little refreshment same as de white folks.

UNCLE JOHN. (*Outside,* R. H.) True, Mr. Jekyl.

POMP. Dat's mas'r; golly! I must keep dark.   (*Exit,* L. H.)

Enter UNCLE JOHN *and Mr.* JEKYL, R. H.

UNCLE JOHN. Yes, sir, yes, Mr. Jekyl. I am a perfect martyr, sir. My wife, Mrs. G., is a good woman, a very good woman; but, sir, she's a downright dragon, sir! She never sleeps; she's always finding out plots, treasons and conspiracies on my plantation; calling down on my devoted head the necessity of discriminations, decisions and settlements—abhorrent, most abhorrent, to an easy man like me.

MR. JEKYL. No doubt, no doubt, Mr. Gordon, but Mrs. Gordon is ever watchful for your interest.

UNCLE JOHN. Watchful! Hang it! I don't quarrel with Mrs. G. for walking the whole night long, or sleeping with her head out of the window, watching the smoke-house; or for stealing out after one o'clock to convict Pomp, or circumvent Cuff, if she only wouldn't bother me with it. Suppose the half of the hams were carried off between two and three, and sold to Abijah Skinflint for rum! I must have my sleep; and if I have to pay for it in ham, why, I'd pay for it in ham— but I must have my sleep.

MR. JEKYL. Nature requires it. We must sleep; that is, some must sleep while others keep wide awake. Now, 'tis easy to see there is a wide-awake manager on your plantation; while on this—ah! the difference is lamentable.

UNCLE JOHN. Indeed. I don't observe it; every thing seems to be going on right. Harry is an excellent overseer.

MR. JEKYL. Ahem! For a nigger and a slave.

UNCLE JOHN. Nigger and slave! Hang it! he's next to white, and knows more than many a free man. Then he loves my little Nina dearly, and, I repeat, is an excellent manager for her.

Enter TOM TIT, R.

TOM TIT. The lunch is on the table, gentlemen.

UNCLE JOHN. Mr. Jekyl, go in; I'll join you presently. (*Exit* JEKYL, R.) Well, Master Tom Tit, the same conceit of yourself as ever, I see.

TOM TIT. Sir, if I didn't keep my head up, de common niggers won't pay me no respect; and you know, sir, I ain't a common nigger.

UNCLE JOHN. (*Markedly.*) That you certainly are not.

TOM TIT. I is naturally above dem; and den Miss Nina and de oder ladies' society has untitted me for dem entirely. Common niggers is my aversion.

UNCLE JOHN. Well, Tom, can you so far overcome your horror for common niggers as to see if you can find Pomp, and send him to me?

TOM TIT. With the greatest pleasure, sir. I consider Pomp a degree above de common; he is your own servant, sir, and must know more than de common black people. Pomp shall shortly be in de presence ob (*sings*) "A fine old Virginia Gentleman," &c., (*and exit,* L. H.)

UNCLE JOHN. Ha! ha! ha! The most singular compound of conceit, ceremony and mirth ever concentrated in one little body, I believe. He is something the same as Mrs. G.; she concentrates several peculiarities—vigilance, economy, watchfulness and everlasting argument.

Enter POMP, L. H., *wiping his mouth.*

Pomp—why, you are soon found! I suppose you were taking care of yourself.

POMP. I was taking little refreshment, mas'r, in de pantry.

UNCLE JOHN. Now, Pomp, I want you to mind what I tell you.

POMP. Yes, sar.

UNCLE JOHN. I think you know that my wife, Mrs. G. is a very economical woman.

POMP. (*Grins.*) Berry ecomical, sar.

UNCLE JOHN. And she is right. Now, Pomp, I want you to go over home as soon as Miss Nina arrives, and say to Mrs. G. I sent you for a ham, some meal, a half-bushel of sweet potatoes, and a few hoe cakes.

POMP. (*Shakes his head.*) Mas'r, missus ain't going to gib me dem tings.

UNCLE JOHN. Yes she will; you must say that they have run a little short here, and Aunt Milly sent you.

POMP. Yah! yah! yah! But sposen missus send ober some body to see; cos I know Aunt Milly don't want no such tings.

UNCLE JOHN. Never mind—any thing for a quiet life. You get the things, and carry them down, right away, to that poor devil's, Cripps', cabin; and be sure you give 'em to old Tiff, and nobody else. If Cripps should get hold of the ham he'd sell it for whiskey. But his wife and children, and that faithful old nigger, Tiff, mustn't be left to starve because Cripps is a drunken scoundrel.

POMP. Yes, mas'r. I see now, mas'r, what you was going to make believe you was going to whip our Jake for dis mornin'; cos missus said he stole de ham, an' mas'r know berry well he didn't steal 'em, cos mas'r make him carry 'em to dem poor white trash. Ah! God bress you, mas'r, you 'blige to tief your own tings, cos missus won't let you take 'em.

UNCLE JOHN. (*Making a blow at him with his cane.*) Get out, you scoundrel. (POMP *runs out*, L. H.) Egad! Pomp says true enough. I am obliged to rob myself to keep Mrs. G. quiet. Now for lunch. I don't think I shall eat my little morsel with less relish because I have filled the stomachs of those poor starving wretches. (*Exit*, R. H.)

SCENE III.—*Interior of CRIPPS' log hut. On one side a poor truckle bed, on the other a fire place. An old table—a chair—a stool—a small old leather hair trunk—a door and window in flat. Discovered: MRS. CRIPPS in bed; FANNY and TEDDY, her children, near her—FANNY seated on a log, at work, TEDDY on foot of the bed; OLD TIFF seated on a very low stool, near the fire, and a rude cradle, like a small canoe, on rockers, near him, with the baby in it; TIFF, with specs on, is darning an old stocking.*

MRS. CRIPPS. (*With a short cough.*) I say, Tiff, do you think he will come?

TIFF. (*Aside.*) How can I tell when a drunken man shall come! (*Aloud.*) Laws, missus, I spees so—I hopes so, because you want him.

MRS. CRIPPS. It's so lonesome—so lonesome! O, the pain and worry, and sickness and suffering I have gone through! O dear! O dear!

TIFF. (*Aside, coming forward.*) Only look dar! and she a Payton, too, one ob de oldest, most respectablest and first families in Ole Virginny, to go and trow herself away upon such poor white trash as John Cripps, a drunken good-for-nothing. But ole Tiff is here. She don't know I is a free man. She tinks I b'long to her; but I don't. Ole mas'r made me free in his will. I hab my free papers safe dar. (*Points to the small trunk.*) But I promise ole mas'r nebber to leave Miss Fanny, an' ole Tiff will keep his word.

MRS. CRIPPS. Always wandering from place to place, never settled, worrying, watching, weary—and all for nothing—for I am worn out, and shall die.

TIFF. O law, no! Lor! Tiff has made you some tea, and you must drink a little, poor lamb. (*Pours some tea from an old tea-pot, which he takes from the hearth, into a cracked cup, and carries it to MRS. CRIPPS.*) It's dredful hard, so it is; but times 'll mend. Dar, sip a little, poor lamb. (*She drinks a little. TIFF puts cup on table, and goes to fire.*) Tiff 'll blow up the fire, cos dar ain't no knowing but we may get someting to cook. (*Stoops down, blows the fire.*) (*Aside*)— Dar ain't a scrap in de house, ceptin' de bit ob chicken I saved for missus. (*Aloud.*) Mas'r may bring some ting—(*aside*)—only whiskey, I spose.

MRS. CRIPPS. O, I wish John would come.

TIFF. (*Blowing at fire.*) Bress de Lord, I is drefful strong in my breff. Lawes, dey might hab used me black smissis. I is kep dis yer chimney going dis many a day.

JOHN CRIPPS. (*Outside, D. F.*) Hollo! Tiff! where are you?

TIFF. Dare mas'r, sure as I'm alive.

Enter CRIPPS, D. F.

MRS. CRIPPS. O John! I'm so glad you're come.

CRIPPS. (*At door.*) Yes, I'm come, sis; I'll talk to you presently. Here, Tiff, lay hold and bring in these things.

TIFF *drags in an old packing case.* CRIPPS *brings in a two gallon demijohn, places it near the table.*

CRIPPS. Now, sis, I have made a pretty good spec this time. You see, the fellow I bought this ere case of bonnets of, says they're the height of fashion. They come from Paris the capital of Europe, and I got 'em for a mere song. (*Takes top off the case, and from it a ridiculously large and extravagantly trimmed bonnet.*) Look at that.

TIFF. (*Takes it, looks at it and puts it on. Half aside.*) Fuss rate for a scare crow.

CRIPPS. There's twenty of 'em altogether—all as handsome as that.

TIFF. Twenty such. If I was to meet one of dis yar, of a dark night, in a grave yard, I should tink I was sent for. Poor missus looking mighty faint; don't wonder; sich bonnets is nuff to skeer a weakly woman into fits.

(*Takes off bonnet and lays it on table.*)

CRIPPS, *who has been turning over things in the case, takes out a hooped skirt; looks at it wonderingly.* TIFF, *after looking at it, takes it from him.*

TIFF. What am de ting, any how? 'pears to me it am a fish net.

CRIPPS. Well, I can't say. I don't know how the derned thing got there.

TIFF. (*In wonder, turns it round and round.*) It must be a eel pot, or some sort of a machine to ketch something in. What am dis kivered up inside! (*Feels the whoop.*) Yes, it am a fish pole split up. I can feel the cane; it must be a ting to ketch fish in.

(*Puts it down on case.*)

CRIPPS. (*Sits at table.*) And now, old woman, we'll have something to eat.

TIFF. Dar ain't nothing in de house to eat. (*Aside.*) Not for you. (*Aloud.*) And besides, missus is too weak to sit up to de table.

CRIPPS. Well, then, hand here the demijohn. (*TIFF hands it with a groan. He drinks from the cup.*) I'll take a drop of comfort and a smoke, any how. And the next time I come home, you old nigger, see you have something for me to eat.

(*Lights pipe with coal of fire, smokes and drinks.*)

TIFF. If I gets enuff for missus and de chil'en I tink I does pretty well.

Cripps. You do, eh! Going to be sassy, eh! (*Drinks.*)

Tiff. No, mas'r, I nebber was, only de truth am—

Cripps. O, none of your sermons. I'll tell you what, p'raps you won't be here long. I heard Ben Dakin say something about Squire Tom Gordon having a claim on you.

(*Drinks and getting drunk.*)

Tiff. Claim on me! Hush! (*Goes to bed, looks at Mrs. C.*) She's asleep, poor lamb. Nobody can't have no claim on me, I have my free papers; but I wouldn't hab missus hear dat for de worl'. Hush!

Cripps. Hush yourself. I say, sis! sis! She's asleep, is she! (*Hiccoughs.*) Hic—so shall I be soon. The shaking of that old wag—gon—hic—makes a fellow—hic—drowsy. I've made a good spec this time, and—hic—I'll go to sleep on it.

(*Drops his head on the table and falls asleep.*)

Tiff. Dar, he's off at last. Now, dar's a sight for a mother and her chil'en. It am too bad! If he was only out of de way; if it would please Heaven to call him fust, but I fear not. Poor soul, she's sick enough. Now, chil'en, you go out and play; don't make no noise. (*Puts the children out, D. F.*) And now Tiff 'll do his washing. (*Takes up some things.*) If ole mas'r could see me now, his har's would stand on end. His own body servant, one ob de real Peytons, a washing de clothes.

(*Goes out door flat, taking with him the hooped skirt and bonnet.*)

Scene IV.—*Exterior of* Cripps' *Log Hut.* Tiff *speaks outside,* R. I. E.

Tiff. I must wash de tings near de do', so if missus wakes up I can tend 'pon her. (*Enters, R. H., with the hooped skirt on, pulling on a bench and wash tub, fixes himself, tucks up sleeves, &c.*) Any how, I make dis ting (*fixing the skirt*) mas'r buy, useful. It am a fust rate apron to keep off de suds. (*Begins to wash.*) De sun is pow'ful hot. I don't see no better use for dem bonnets dan to keep off de sun. (*Goes to wing, brings bonnet, puts it on, stands at tub washing, with his back to R. H. Sings.*)

> "If you get dar before I do,
> I'm bound for de land of Canaan."

Gosh! dis spot won't wash out. (*Rubs it, sings.*)

> "Look out for me, I'm coming too,
> I'm bound for de land of Canaan!"

Dis yer is de wustest shirt I ebber see. I is a good mind not to wash a shirt for sich as he, sich white trash, but den he is missuses husband, and she is a Peyton—and I is a Peyton, too. (*Washes—singing.*)

> "Look out for me, I'm coming too,
> I'm bound for de land of Canaan."

Enter Pomp, R. H., *with covered basket.*

Pomp. Eh! who am dat! Ole Tiff mus' be hired some woman to do de washin. What a bonnet! Dat am de most distractedest looking bonnet ebber dis chile see! An' what ebber under de sun am dat ting he stan' up in! Am it a barrel, or a sugar hogshead, or what am it!

1*

TIFF. (*His back to* POMP, *sings.*)

"My way is dark and cloudy,
    So it is, so it is;
My way is dark and cloudy,
    All dis day!"

(*Accompanying each word or two with a rub at the clothes.*)

POMP. Why, it can't be possible dat am Tiff, his-self!

(*Sings the same hymn.*)

" But we'll jine de forty tousand, by-an-by,
    So we will, so we will."

(TIFF *turns round—both singing together.*)

" We'll jine de forty tousand 'pon de golden shore,
    An' our sorrows will be gone, for ever more, more, more.

(*They both look at each other.*)

POMP. It am Tiff, by de laws!

TIFF. To be sure it am. You see I does dis yer little washin'; 'cos a Peyton orter be able to do ebbery ting.

POMP. Yes, de Peytons am some; but dar am one ting de Peytons can't do.

TIFF. I should like to know what am dat one ting.

POMP. Dat *one* ting, am eatiug! and dat de Peytons can't do *widout.*

TIFF. (*Pulls off specs—rubs them.*) Dat am a fact.

POMP. So, in case any ob de family might want dat one ting dey can't do widout, why, dere is some ting in dis basket dat is good for de Peytons' insides, or anybody's insides.

TIFF. (*Takes basket—looks in it.*) Who send it?

POMP. I was to say, missus; an' if I say missus, an' missus ever find it out, den dis child is a gone coon.

TIFF. (*With an air.*) Nigger, who present dis!

POMP. Squire John Gordon.

TIFF. Squire John Gordon's one ob de ole Virginny blood. De oldest family in Virginny can accept a present from Squire John. (*Pompously.*) Nigger, clar away dese tings out yonder. (*Points to wash-bench, &c.; then to* R. H. POMP *hesitates.*)

TIFF. (*Draws himself up, puts on his specs, and looks at him.*) Clar de tings! If I condescends to wash for de daughter ob de Peytons, I dosn't clar de kitchen. (*Waves his hand.*) Clar de kitchen, I say! (POMP *removes bench, &c., off* R., *and exits.*)

TIFF. If I demeans myself for de Peytons, I don't let common niggers make too free. (*Peeps in at* D. F.) He is asleep. Now to hide away dese tings for missus an' de children. He shan't hab a taste—no, not a smell. *He* am a Cripps. Dese are for de Peytons. (*Exit, with basket, into hut.*)

SCENE V.—*Exterior of the Mansion. Same as* 1st *Scene, this Act.*

Enter from house, R., TOM TIT. (*He calls off,* L. H.) Here, niggers! niggers!

Enter CUFF *and all the negroes.* L. H. U. E.

Old. What am it!

Tom Tit. Niggers, be ready. I have been observationing from de pupulo on de pinnacle ob de mansion, and in de prospective distance ob de horizon I distinguish Ole Hundred, de family coachman, driving de carriage ob Miss Nina.

All. Hurrah! Hurrah!

Tom Tit. Away, den, and meet de female representative ob de Gordons wid all de pomps and wanities of dis glorious occasion. Away! (*All exeunt*, L. H. *shouting.*)

Enter UNCLE JOHN *and* MR. JEKYL, *from house.*

Tom Tit. (*Bows, crosses to house.*) I go to announce de speedy approach of Miss Nina, to de ole lady, her aunt.

(*Bows. Exit into house.*)

UNCLE JOHN. Nina 's coming at last, eh! Well, Mr. Jekyl, I must say, on this subject I disagree with you entirely. Harry is an uncommon specimen. He is a bold, respectful, intelligent, industrious fellow, and the very main stay of this plantation and my dear Nina's interests. If he was her brother, he couldn't love her better, or do more for her.

Loud Shouts. U. E. L.

Hurrah for Harry! Harry for ever!

UNCLE JOHN. You hear that about for Harry! There's not a nigger on the plantation that does not respect or fear him. He is a fine fellow, is Harry, and here he comes. (*Enter,* U. E. L. HARRY, *dressed in a complete suit of white—straw hat, patent leather boots and gloves.*

UNCLE JOHN. How d'ye do, Harry! Glad to see you. My little Nina arrived yet!

HARRY. Miss Gordon is expected every minute, sir. Hearing you were here, I came to pay my respects, and, in my mistress' name, bid you welcome to Canema, and ask if you would please to take any refreshment after your ride.

UNCLE JOHN. (*To* MR. JEKYL.) What do you say to that! Isn't that about the right thing!

MR. JEKYL. (*To him.*) He knows what he's about—cunning rascal.

HARRY. (*Aside—looking at* JEKYL) That man, to me, has a most forbidding appearance. My flesh crawls at his sight.

UNCLE JOHN. We have had refreshments; thank you, Harry. (*Introduces.*) Mr. Jekyl, Mr. Tom Gordon's man of law.

HARRY. (*Bows. Aside.*) Tom Gordon; that accounts for my feelings. May I ask, sir, if Mr. Tom Gordon is expected here soon!

MR. JEKYL. You may ask, sir, but I do not choose to answer. Lawyers are not too communicative.

HARRY. Beg pardon, sir. (*Aside.*) I knew he was a brute. There is a gentleman has met with an accident, has been thrown from his horse. He inquired for his uncle, Mr. Jekyl.

MR. JEKYL. Ah! that must be my nephew, Mr. Cipher Cute, now studying law with me. Where is he!

HARRY. I assisted him out of the swamp, sir, and directed some of the people to show him this way to the house.

CIPHER CUTE. (*Speaks outside*, L. H. U. E.) That 'll do, you can quit neow. I see uncle's horse—I'm all right neow.

MR. JEKYL. That's my nephew's voice. Here he comes.

Enter U. E. L., CIPHER CUTE, *in a very short-tailed white coatee, striped homespun pants, very short, with straps, shoes and striped stockings; straw hat, with very broad black crape band round it. He is muddied all over, his hat crushed, &c.*

CIPHER. Dod darn the cussed crettur's hide, I say.

MR. JEKYL. What's the matter, nephew! How came you in this pickle!

CIPHER. Pickle! derned strong pickle tew, I guess. Heow came I intew it! I'll tell you beow. Just as I came reound the turn at the eend of the big swamp you told me of, where the niggers run away and hide in; wal, just as I turned the corner, eout jumps a big buck nigger, black as the ace of spades, in a red flannel shirt, his neck like a bull's, and his arms naked; he throws 'em high in the air, and yells eout, "Beware! Return to thine own people! Listen not to him who would teach thee; justice is only for the white man!" Then he gin a yell like the bull of Bashan; you might have heard it from Maine to Georgy, and vanished intew the swamp head-first, and my tarnal crittur of a horse vamoosed in tew, tail first.

MR. JEKYL. That must have been Dred of the Dismal Swamp. There's a fine specimen of your educated nigger. Religious, too; can find you half a dozen warrants in Scripture for cutting the same number of white people's throats. He's a true son of his father, Denmark Vesey, who headed the bloody insurrection of the niggers in South Carolina; like him, he's a religious enthusiast, and like him, I doubt not, is in communication with *other educated* niggers on plantations not a hundred miles from here. (*Looks at Harry.*)

UNCLE JOHN. I should hope not; their own sense should show them the imprudence, not to say criminality, of holding communication with such an outlaw.

MR. JEKYL. We shall see; time will show. Squire Gordon, allow me to introduce my nephew, Mr. Cipher Cute.

CIPHER. Of the Cutes of Connetticut, formerly of Massachusetts, and hull soul'd right deown patriots. Helped tew plant the tree of liberty in Bosting, and start all the tea in tew the river.

UNCLE JOHN. (*Aside, bowing stiffly.*) Low fellow.

CIPHER. Uncle Judas, want tew know what that crittur, Dred, 's outlawed for!

MR. JEKYL. For running away from his master, and for aiding and abetting other slaves to do the same; and now, it's pretty well known, endeavoring to stir up other slaves to revolt.

CIPHER. Re-volt! That's tew syllables of *our* revolution. Want tew know if the men that stirred up our revolution was educated or ignorant? Seems tew me, Uncle Judas, if I'm studying law in order tew meet eout justice, 'tis but right I should cipher this eout. Uncle Judas, you know the Cute's was allers for ciphering things eout right. Neow, I want tew know what you call educated niggers!

MR. JEKYL. Those that are taught to read and write; that always makes them dangerous.

Cipher. Heow so !

Mr. Jekyl. Why, don't you see what dangerous weapons you put into their hands. They spread their knowledge; bright smart niggers will pick it up; for, the very fellows who are most dangerous are the very ones who'll be sure to learn.

Cipher. Jist so; and what harm if they do !

Mr. Jekyl. What harm ! You are yet a stranger to this part of the country, or you wouldn't ask such a question.

Cipher. This part of the country ! Isn't all this country the United States ! Isn't the same Heaven over this part of the country as over any other part of the country ! Don't the stars and stripes float over this part of the country and over all "The land of the free and the home of the brave !" Want tew know.

Harry. (*Aside.*) The question, the question; "my heart asks it."

Uncle John. Mr. Jekyl, it appears to me, the first portion of your nephew's studies should be to obtain a thorough knowledge of our Southern institutions, and then he would understand his subject better, and talk in a very different strain. He is a little too democratic for us.

Cipher. Democratic ! Guess I be. I'm one of the people, one of the working class.

Uncle John. So I perceive; one of the educated democracy of the North; I don't like 'em. (*Crosses to* r. h.)

Cipher. (*Ironically.*) You don't ! They must feel awful bad at that.

Mr. Jekyl. (*Aside to him.*) Hush ! you'll ruin yourself.

Uncle John. Yes, I repeat, sir, I don't like 'em. What do working-men want with education ! Education ruins 'em, sir, ruins 'em. I have heard of their learned blacksmiths bothering round, neglecting their work to make speeches. I don't like such things. It raises them above their station.

Cipher. Above their station ! I want tew know !

Mr. Jekyl. Hush ! I say.

Uncle John. Above their station. And there's nothing going on up in those Northern states but a constant confusion and hubbub. All sorts of heresies come from the North—Angel Gabriels, infidelity, abolitionism, and the Lord knows what. We have peace down here; and I advise you, Mr. Jekyl, so to school this person that he may not introduce any of his Northern fanatical notions, subversive of order, peace and Southern liberty. Sir, Southern liberty ! (*Exit into house.*)

Mr. Jekyl. Confound your ciphering. Cipher me this—Have you any money !

Cipher. No.

Mr. Jekyl. Do you hope to make some !

Cipher. Guess I do.

Mr. Jekyl. And do you expect to make it by displeasing every one, driving away my clients, and gathering more of your own !

Cipher. No.

Mr Jekyl. Then learn the difference between Southern and Northern liberty, and black and white. Till then, keep your mouth shut. I must after the Squire and talk him over. Cipher Cute, if you would remain with me and feather your nest, do as I do, or I'll pack you off North again, as poor as you came.   (*Exit into house.*)

CIPHER. Oh, git eout! a man mustn't say his soul's his own. Here's a breeze! I say, stranger, you helped me out of the swamp, can you help me to cipher this eout—What's right North's wrong South, eh!

HARRY. Sir, I may have an opinion, but it would not become a slave to express it.

CIPHER. A slave! Be you a slave!

HARRY. I am. I belong to Miss Nina Gordon and this plantation.

CIPHER. (Whistles.) Phew. (Looks at him.) Want tew know. And can you read and write!

HARRY. Both, sir.

CIPHER. And what does your reading teach you! Speak eout. I'm a man, so are you. So, man tew man, and eout with it.

HARRY. Sir, you are a stranger to me, but the free expression of your own sentiments but now, emboldens me to utter mine. I will speak the truth, and only the truth; and if that is wrong, and brings punishment on me, why 'tis the will of Heaven, and I submit. Then, sir, I will trouble you with—

(*Distant shouts outside*, L. H.)

Hark! that shout announces the arrival of Miss Nina, my dear young mistress. Another time, sir; I must now hasten to meet her.

(*Exit*, L. U. E.)

(UNCLE JOHN, *inside the house*.)

UNCLE JOHN. That is my dear Nina.

(*Enter from house* UNCLE JOHN, MRS. NESBIT, *the* REV. OBADIAH OR-THODOX, MR. JEKYL, *followed by* AUNT MILLY.)

(*Shouts again, louder*, L. H.)

(TOM TIT *rushes down the steps from the house*, R. H., *clapping his hands and shouting, tumbles against the* REV. ORTHODOX, *nearly upsets him, picks himself up in a minute, sings*, "*Out of the way, old Dan Tucker*," *and runs out*, L. H. U. E., *singing*, "*Oh, I is going to glory*.")

ORTHODOX. Verily, my equilibrium was endangered.

MRS. NESBIT. (Holds up her hand.) Sinful little wretch. No respect, no respect.

UNCLE JOHN. (Laughs.) Never mind, Father Orthodox, love for his young mistress made him forgetful.

JEKYL. Love of mischief.

ORTHODOX. (Groans.) They are a dark and hardened generation.

CIPHER. Who's Shovel Hat! A minister, I guess.

(*Loud shouts. Enter in procession. All the negroes, headed by* TOM TIT, *singing the opening chorus. Then enter* NINA GORDON *and* HARRY, *followed by* OLD HUNDRED, *the coachman, with whip, &c., and* CUFF, *literally covered with bundles, band-boxes, &c.*)

NINA. (*Embraces* UNCLE JOHN.) My dear, dear Uncle John, how good of you to come and welcome me home.

UNCLE JOHN. My dear little Nina, bless you! bless you! (*Kisses her forehead.*)

NINA. My dear aunt Nesbit. (*Kisses her and embraces her warmly.*)

MRS. NESBIT. My dear niece—there, child—moderate your transports.

NINA. I can't be moderate; my joy won't let me. I could hug and kiss everybody.

ORTHODOX. Everybody—oh!

TOM TIT. Dat's what de Scriptures tells us—everybody loves everybody.

(*He motions to CUFF to bring the things to the house. CUFF lets fall a bundle. and puts down a band-box to pick it up.*)

TOM TIT. Please stand out of de way, (*to* ORTHODOX,) sir, and let de nigger deposit de packages in de proper receptacle.

ORTHODOX *steps back, and falls into the band box.* AUNT MILLY *helps him up.* TOM TIT *holds up the smashed hat.*

AUNT MILLY. (*To* TOM TIT.) You see what you have done.

NINA. Ah! one of my new opera hats.

ORTHODOX. I opine my weight is unfavorable to its construction. 'Twas not my fault; 'twas that young—young—Verily, my wrath rises. I dare not utter what I would say.

TOM TIT. (*Puts on the hat. Sings, as exits into house.*) Oh, I'm going to glory! de, doo, dar, &c.

MRS. NESBIT. Going to glory, oh!

ORTHODOX. Oh! (*Goes up.*)

MR. JEKYL *seems to converse with* MRS. NESBIT. *They are up-stage.*

NINA. (*Laughs.*) Tom Tit is the same as ever, I see; but he must be forgiven. There must be no scolding, or any fault found this day. Must there, Uncle John?

UNCLE JOHN. No, my little Nina, except by myself.

NINA. And everybody knows your scolding don't amount to much.

UNCLE JOHN. I never tried it on you yet. I am going to do so now.

NINA. Go ahead, then, as we say North.

UNCLE JOHN. North! Don't speak the word. It's well for you he don't belong to the North. You shouldn't have him if he did.

NINA. Have him! Have who?

UNCLE JOHN. Come, come, Miss Puss; I've heard all about it. You're engaged; you can't deny it.

NINA. I don't. I am; and to no less than *three* beaux.

UNCLE JOHN. Three!

NINA. Three. (*Spells it.*) T-h-r-e-e.

UNCLE JOHN. (*Whistles.*) The dev—— the old boy!

NINA. Yes; but I only intend to have one of 'em—and perhaps none.

UNCLE JOHN. I've only heard of one.

NINA. And his name is—

UNCLE JOHN. Edward Clayton—one of us—a neighbor—a fine fellow, barring one or two little peculiarities; but he has my consent.

NINA. (*Curtsies.*) Thank you, Uncle—when I ask it. Pray who put this absurd nonsense into your head!

UNCLE JOHN. (*Points to* JEKYL.) He; your brother Tom's man of law; and let me tell you, my little Nina, your brother Tom doesn't like Clayton a bit, and he is raging about it.

NINA. Let him. I promise you, when necessary, I shall consult my own inclinations only. I am Gordon enough for that; and while I have Harry here as my manager, I can do without any other male creature—at least at present. But, Harry, what makes you look so solemn! You are calculating the amount of those dreadful bills, for all the finery I purchased up in New-York, eh?

HARRY. (*Who has been looking over a number of bills.*) I was calculating, Miss Nina, some time time or other—perhaps soon—you will marry; you ought. You need somebody to take care of the property and place.

NINA. O, that's it; is it! You are tired of keeping accounts with me to spend the money. And what's the use of keeping accounts! When money is spent, it is spent; isn't it, Uncle John! and keeping accounts ever so strict won't bring it back again. I am very careful about my expenses. I never get any thing that I can do without.

HARRY. (*Smiles.*) For instance: this bill of one hundred dollars for confectionary.

NINA. Well, you know just how it is. It's so horrid to have to study. Girls must have something; and you know, Uncle, I didn't get it all for myself; I gave it round to all the girls. They used to ask me for it, and I couldn't refuse, and so it went.

HARRY. I didn't presume to comment, Miss Nina. What have we here! Madame Les Cartes, $450.

UNCLE JOHN. Phew! $450!

NINA. O, Uncle! that horrid Madame Les Cartes! You never saw any thing like her. Positively, it is not my fault. She puts down things I never get. I know she does. Nothing in the world but because she comes from Paris. Everybody is complaining of her. But, then, nobody gets any thing any where else. So, what can we do, you know. I assure you I am very economical.

HARRY *and* UNCLE JOHN *laugh.*

NINA. Harry, now, for shame! Positively you are not respectful. Uncle, if you laugh, I'll pull your ear.

Enter, at porch, TOM TIT, *ringing a large bell.*

TOM TIT. De banquet ob de choicest delicacies ob de season is served in de saloon for we gentlefolks; and de tables groan under de weight ob de hog and hominy for de common niggers.

MUSIC. Opening chorus repeated. To which NINA, *with* UNCLE JOHN *on one side and* HARRY *on the other, enter the house, bowed in by* TOM TIT. *Then* ORTHODOX *and* MRS. NESBIT *and* JEKYL; OLD HUNDRED, *with much ceremony, hands in* AUNT MILLY. CIPHER *is down in one corner,* L. II.; TOM TIT *advances to him very ceremoniously, eyes him from top to toe; at length he offers* CIPHER *his arm, which he takes— they exeunt into the house.*

POMP. (*And all the niggers laugh.*) Now den, niggers, de plantation jig; den for de hog and de hominy.

PLANTATION JIG.—*Air, " Pop goes the Weasle." At the conclusion* Tom Tit *re-enters—dances in the centre.* Pomp *and* Cuff *hoist him up on their shoulders—all shout. Drop descends on*

ANIMATED PICTURE.

ACT II.

SCENE I.—*A handsome apartment, with wine, &c., on table; a door open, looking out on to the garden or plantation;* FRANK RUSSELL, *lolling on a sofa, smoking a cigar;* CLAYTON *at table.*

CLAYTON. I cannot help it, Frank; I certainly shall not be deterred in carrying out my own plans for the improvement of the condition of my own slaves, by such men as Tom Gordon.

RUSSELL. But, my dear fellow, your notions of slavery will keep you out of the world. As a lawyer, you'll never get a case; you'll be nothing but an insignificant country gentleman, rusticating all his life on his plantation.

CLAYTON. Not insignificant, if I can bestow the blessings of education and improvement on hundreds of my fellow creatures, whom Providence has been pleased to place under my control.

(*Large bell rings outside.*)

RUSSELL. What's that?

CLAYTON. My sister Ann's school-bell. Now you shall see her scholars. I have directed them to pass in review before us, as they go home from school. This is a practical demonstration of my plans.

MUSIC.—*Symphony to the school children's chorus. To which enter centre doors, all the Magnolia Grove School Children, two and two—the girls are in homespun frocks, with long sleeves, with aprons and white handkerchiefs or capes, and Bandana handkerchiefs on their heads; the boys in homespun jackets and trowsers, white aprons, and white collars turned down, and straw hats—they pass around the whole stage singing thus :*

"The blessings of edu-ca-tion,
        The blessings of edu-ca-tion.
Make us happy on mas're plan-ta-tion,
And carry freedom throughout a nation,
        A nation, a na-tion,
And carry freedom throughout a nation."

This repeated, if necessary, until they all file out at a doors again. The girls all curtsey and boys bow, as they pass CLAYTON *and* RUSSELL.

CLAYTON. There, sir, in those simple words those children sing, I place my trust of the future. Through the blessings of education, they will be all led to ultimate freedom.

RUSSELL. And e'er that time arrives, our children's children—that is, may be yours will be pursuing the same course—and the negroes will be precisely in the same position they are now. Come, man, live for the present; plunge into political life, and be somebody.

CLAYTON. I cannot—my conscience will not permit me.

RUSSELL. (*Laughing.*) Ha! ha! ha! Conscience! I say with Iago,
"a fig for conscience. It is in ourselves that we are thus or thus."

CLAYTON. I'm like the minister in his own village, who married
a pretty little girl, and when the elders came to inquire if she had the
requisite qualifications for a pastor's wife, he told them he didn't think
she had. But, said he, the fact is, if she is not quite a saint, she's a
very pretty little sinner, and I love her. That's precisely my case.

RUSSELL. Very sensibly said.

CLAYTON. And I believe—I'm quite sure—that I'm the only person
in the world that ever touched her heart at all. I am not sure she
loves me now, but I am quite sure she will.

RUSSELL. Hum! they say that she is generally engaged to two or
three at a time. I say, old fellow, don't go in beyond your depth.

CLAYTON. Too late—I am in.

RUSSELL. Well, then, good luck to you, my dear fellow. But now
the substantials—the—

CLAYTON. What do you mean!

RUSSELL. Why, her estates, man, her estates.

CLAYTON. Not far from my own, but nothing very considerable.
Managed nominally by an old uncle of hers, uncle John Gordon, but
really by a very clever quadroon slave, who was left her by her
father, and who has received an education, and has talents very superior to what are usually allotted to those in this class. He is, in
fact, the overseer of her plantation, and I believe Harry to be the
most loyal devoted creature breathing.

(TOM TIT, *heard without*, L. H.)

TOM. Don't interrupt me, common nigger; stand out of the way.

CLAYTON. What now—who have we here!

(*Enter* TOM TIT, L., *he bows very ceremoniously.* CLAYTON *returns it,*
looking at RUSSELL *and laughing.*)

CLAYTON. Pray, sir, may I ask what you are!

TOM. Sir, I don't make it a practice to indulge vulgar curiosity, but,
sir, (*bows low,*) to do real gentlemen, like Mr. Clayton, which I presume
you are.

CLAYTON. (*Bows.*) At your service.

TOM. I is always willing to make myself known. I am, sir, Mr.
Tom Tit, one of de Gordons of Canema.

CLAYTON. This is a character. Oh, you are one of the Gordons, and
pray, Mr. Tom Tit, to what am I to attribute the honor of this visit!

TOM. De honor ob dis visit, sir, proceed from this. (*Takes out*
letter, hands it.) I am, I believe, love's messenger.

RUSSELL. Love's messenger, eh! (*Looks at* Clayton.) Oh, ho! then
you come from Miss Nina Gordon!

TOM. I have that honor, dat is, I come from her house, but dat letter is from Mr. John Gordon, her uncle.

CLAYTON. Russell, excuse me a few moments.   (*Exit* L. H.)

TOM. (*With surprise.*) Is that the polished Mr. Clayton!

RUSSELL. Yes, why do you ask!

Tom. He don't show his broughtings up, to offer a young lady's messenger no kind of refreshment.

Russell. Mr. Tit, permit me to make up for the lack of courtesy in my friend, Mr. Clayton; you know love, Mr. Tom, drives every thing else out of the head.

Tom. (*Sighs.*) Ah, it does, indeed. I don't exactly speak from experience, but I intend to very shortly.

Russell. You do.

Tom. Yes, I have serious thoughts of falling in love.

Russell. Ha! ha! ha!

Tom. In the mean time, I have no objection to fall in with something more substantial.

Russell. This way, Mr. Tit.

(*Ceremony of who shall go first, at length* Tom *does.* Russell *follows, laughing,* R. H.)

CHANGE SCENE.

Scene II.—*Front wood. Enter* Jekyl *and* Tom Gordon.

Tom. I tell you every thing is going to the devil, and I won't put up with it. To be sure, the plantation isn't mine yet, but one day it may be, and I won't let it be ruined by the folly of a sister, and the mismanagement of a confounded nigger.

Jekyl. While your sister Nina is single you may have something to say, but when she marries—

Tom. Ay, when she does. I don't intend she shall.

Jekyl. How are you to prevent it? she is her own mistress.

Tom. Is she? we will see that, never mind how I'll prevent, but I will do it. I say she shan't marry, and more particularly that fellow, Clayton. He is a traitor to the South, and I'll prove it yet, and make this part of the country too hot to hold him. But now, have you those papers relating to that runaway vagabond, old Tiff?

Jekyl. I have sent my nephew for them.

Tom. There's a canting old scoundrel, now, that has been my property for years, though the law, through one of your cheating tribe, has kept him away from me. Now, however, you say you can prove he is my property.

Jekyl. Most certainly.

Tom. And you know where he is?

Jekyl. The poor white wretch, John Cripps, who married Miss Peyton, Tiff's mistress, has squatted down on your and John's plantation.

Tom. And he shelters the hound, and all his family, I suppose. Well, he may do as he will with the white trash, but I must have my nigger, my own property. I have a purchaser for him as soon as I can get possession.

Ben Dakin. (*Outside,* L. H.) Come, hurry up, or I'll be down on some of you.

(*Enter a number of slaves, male and female, in wretched attire, manacled, driven in by* Ben *with a heavy whip.*)

Ben Dakin *to* Tom. Ah! squire, glad to see you in this part of the country. We want somebody to look round a little, and keep things as they ought to be, or we shan't have a nigger left.

TOM. How so?

BEN. Why, they'll all be off to the swamp.

TOM. Ah! What! Is that fellow, Dred, not hunted out yet?

BEN. No, nor never will be while he's protected.

TOM. Protected! Protected by whom!

BEN. Well, I ain't no right just exactly to say by who. I has my thoughts.

TOM. So have I mine.

BEN. Well, its your business now to hunt after one of your own niggers. Old Jem, as you gave me to sell amongst my lot, he's off to the swamp.

TOM. What! run away?

BEN. Yes; he cut this morning from the coffle, but I'll soon be on his track with my dogs; they know him—they've smelt his clothes; only let them get scent of that old long-skirted, homespun coat of his, and they'll hang on to him like grim death.

TOM. My nigger Jem, sh!—worth $500, off to the swamp; spirited away by that outlaw—that psalm-singing villain, Dred! This comes of teaching niggers to read. But I'll soon put a stop to it, or my name's not Tom Gordon.

BEN. That's right, squire, I'm on hand any time to help in that. I'm just going to show this lot to Father Brune, a customer of mine, then come back to pen them up in the coffle, and then I'm on old Jem's track with my dogs. I'll take him alive if I can.

TOM. Do so. You have my authority to take him, dead or alive. And harkee, Ben, come to Canema, and let me know how you succeed. I have some other business on hand for you.

BEN. Ay, ay, squire; I'll be there after the hunt. Come, move on niggers, be lively!

(Drives out the niggers, R. H.)

TOM. A pretty pass things have come to when we can't keep our own niggers—they must be coaxed off to the swamp—run away from us. And we must lose our property, and bear it. This is Clayton's doings. We never had half these troubles till he came to live here.

CLAYTON. (*Outside,* L.) Lead my horse round. I'll walk through the wood.

TOM. Talk of the devil, and he is here.

JEKYL. Be patient; keep the law on your side.

TOM. When I want your advice I'll ask it.

JEKYL. I'll be in the way, and only see and hear what I ought, in case of being called on as a witness. (*Exit,* R. H.)

(Enter CLAYTON, L.)

TOM. Well met, sir.

CLAYTON. If you say so, perhaps.

TOM. I do say so. There's nothing like plain speaking. I have only a few words to say. I know you, Mr. Clayton.

*(*CLAYTON *bows.*)

TOM. Yes, sir, I know you for one that despises the institutions of his country; one that tramples on them, sir; one who knows no distinction between black and white—or if he does, it is rather in favor of the former—whom he considers a down-trodden and oppressed race, and thinks it an honor to champion.

CLAYTON. Sir, my considerations and thoughts are my own, and subject to no man's challenge.

TOM. But the effects of them are; and your acts are, sir. The system of education you have introduced amongst the negroes on your plantation is subversive of the good management of all your neighbors—introduces insubordination, and may lead to insurrection, sir—insurrection.

CLAYTON. I cannot see that the greatest blessing man can be endowed with, education, can lead to such results.

TOM. No you can't, nor none of your blinded, fanatical race. I know you, sir.

CLAYTON. And, I'm sorry to say, I know you, sir.

TOM. What do you know of me, sir?

CLAYTON. I know you, sir, for a man whom nature has endowed with no mean share of talents, but which have been most shamefully abused. Brought up from infancy among slaves, to whom his will was law; disdaining the reins of authority, though held by the hands of parents, you early threw off all restraint; rapidly acquiring the knowledge of Bowie knives, revolvers and vicious literature, and ultimately bringing a father's gray hairs with sorrow to the grave. You see I know you, sir.

TOM. And shall know more of me before we part. Hark'ee, sir. Will you fight?

CLAYTON. (*Lifting his hat and crosses, R. H.*) Not with Nina Gordon's brother. (*Exit R. H.*)

(*Enter CIPHER, L, his back towards TOM GORDON; he runs against him.*)

TOM. Stand out of my way, fellow. (*Going.*)

CIPHER. Fellow, yourself. How do you like it?

TOM. (*Returns.*) What do you mean by that?

CIPHER. The same to you.

TOM. The same what?

CIPHER. Sarse.

TOM. How?

CIPHER. Heow? Why, what's sarse for the goose is sarse for the gander. You fellowed me, and I fellowed you.

TOM. Pshaw! (*Going off, L. H.*)

CIPHER. Say! look a here! come back.

TOM. Well, sir, what is it?

CIPHER. Wal, not much, only I wouldn't have a misunderstanding—on our first acquaintance you called me fellow.

TOM. I did. What then?

CIPHER. Wal—I wouldn't have you go away under a misapprehension. Remember, I am no fellow of yours.

TOM. Pshaw! Fool!   (*Exit, L. H.*)

CIPHER. Fool! Say! (*Calls.*) Look in the first brook you come to and you'll see a derned sight bigger one. That chap looks now as if he

could swallow a nigger, hide, boots and toe nails, without salt.   Hello!
Who comes here?—a gang of chained niggers—human property held
under difficulties, I guess.

Enter BEN DAKIN *and gang,* R.

OLD NIGGER. (*Very lame, with foot tied up in bloody rag.*)   Do,
Massa Ben, honey, do, let dis child get a drink of water—my foot
pains me.

BEN. Well, you shouldn't have run away, and then the dogs wouldn't
have held on to you.   I ain't got no time to let you be running after
water.

CIPHER. (*To old nigger.*) Say, daddy, how would a little of this do
for your complaint?   (*Shows flask.*)   Take a horn—it's real Bourbon.
                                                  (*Nigger drinks.*)

BEN. Real Bourbon!   Is it?   Shouldn't mind 'bout tasting of it
myself.

CIPHER. You'll have it—in a horn.

BEN. No; my mouth—my measure—it holds just a comfortable
swallow.

CIPHER. Does it?   Then I guess that's the only comfortable thing
you have about you. If you get a drink out of me it will be in a horn.

SONG.

" Yankee doodle, he's the chap
    Cries freedom in every station,
    But all the freedom for the whites
    The blacks——may see tarnation."

SCENE III. — *Exterior of* HARRY's *Log Hut.   Bulle rue Plantation.
        Music.*   LISSETTE *from Log Hut,* L. H.

LISS. How surprised Harry will be when he sees the little feast I
have prepared for him on his birthday.   He is so full of business,
especially since Miss Nina has been away, that he has not ever thought
of this being his birthday.   Oh! I wish he'd come.   Hark! I hear
horses' hoofs.   (*Runs up.*)   Yes, yes, 'tis he.   (*Enter* HARRY, R. U. E.)
Harry! Harry! you're come at last!   I am so glad; and tell me if
Miss Nina's come home!

HARRY. Yes, Lissette; and she has brought a beautiful present for
you, which you are to come over to the plantation and receive from
her own hands.

LISS. What is it, Harry, what is it?   Oh! do tell me.

HARRY. I don't know, indeed.   But I do know what my own is.
Can you guess?

LISS. No, indeed.   What is it? do tell me quick—quick.

HARRY. Patience! Patience!   (*Takes out a gold watch.*)

LISS. (*Clasps her hands and jumps for joy.*) A gold watch! and
what a beauty!   Oh, I'd think, Harry, we are the most fortunate people—you and I, Harry.   Every thing goes just as we want it—don't
it, now?

HARRY. (*Sighs heavily.*) It appears so to you.

Liss. Why, Harry, what is the matter with you? Why don't you rejoice as I do?

Harry. Oh, Lissette, I have a very perplexing business to manage. Miss Nina is a dear, good little mistress, but she don't know any thing about accounts or money; and here she has brought me home a set of bills to settle, and I'm sure I don't know where the money is to come from. It's hard work to make the old place profitable in our days; and then those bills which Miss Nina brings from New-York are perfectly frightful.

Liss. Well, Harry, what are you going to do? You always know how to do something.

Harry. Why, Lissette, I shall have to do what I have done two or three times before—take the money I have saved, to pay those bills—our freedom money, Lissette. But now, here it is, just as the sum is almost made up, I must pay out five hundred dollars of it, and that throws us back two or three years longer.

Liss. Harry, what makes you love Miss Nina so much?

Harry. Now, Lissette, I will answer that; but you must promise me, most sacredly, that the secret shall be lodged in your own bosom, never to be revealed.

Liss. Harry, I promise. By that power above, which you have taught me to love and worship, I swear it.

Harry. Nina Gordon is my sister.

Liss. Harry!

Harry. Yes, Lissette, I am Colonel Gordon's eldest son. Let me say so once, if I never dare utter it again.

Liss. Harry, who told you?

Harry. He—my father—he himself told me when he was dying, and charged me always to watch over her—my sister—and I have done it. I never told Miss Nina. I wouldn't have told her for the world. But I feel, Lissette, that I have the family blood and the family pride—but what to do with it. I feel that I am a Gordon. I feel in my very heart that I am like Colonel Gordon; I know I am. I look like him; and that's the reason why Tom Gordon always hated me. And then to have a sister—a dear sister—to feel, to know she's my sister, but never dare to utter a word of it. Ah, she little thinks, when she plays and jokes with me, how I feel. Tom Gordon treats her like a brute; and yet he must have all the position, all the respect. And then she often says to me, by way of apology for his brutality, "Ah, you know, Harry, he is the only brother I have in the world." Oh, it is too bad, too bad; more than man can bear. And this curse of slavery is on me, and on you, my wife, and on our children and children's children for ever. Slavery must be the fate of every child of mine. And yet people say, "You have all you want; why are you not happy?" I only wish they could try. Do they think that broadcloth coats can comfort a man for all this? But what can we do?   (*Chord.*)

Enter suddenly, at back, c, Dred.

Dred. Do! What does the wild horse do? Launch out our hoofs, rear up and come down upon them. What does the rattlesnake? Lie in their path and bite. Why did they make slaves of us? They tried the wild Indian first; why didn't they keep to them? They wouldn't be slaves, and we will. They that will bear the yoke, may bear it. (*Shouts at distance—gun fires.*) Hark! the hunt is up. Human blood is the scent—the dogs track another victim. Harry, the destroyer is near—watch! watch! where your heart's ties are closest bound, look for the blow to fall (*Shouts and baying of dogs at a distance.*) Hark! the bloodhounds would dye their fangs once more in our brothers' blood! Up Dred! up and away! ©

(*Music. Rushes out as scene closes.*)

SCENE IV.—*Front wood—half dark—thunder and rain heard. Enter* BEN DAKIN *and* BIGE SKINFLINT, R.

BEN. I tell ye, Bige, my dogs never open their heads if they ain't on the right track. Didn't I give one this ere piece of the very coat old Jem wears to smell of! No, no, they're on the track—we shall have him.

BIGE. If he don't head for the swamp. And then if he does, I'll bet you a quart of whiskey Dred hides him away.

BEN. And I say, Bige, old fellow, who helps Dred to powder and ball and whiskey; besides you don't, do you! (*Sneeringly.*)

BIGE. Ben Dakin—I makes my living my way, by selling groceries, and other things, and you makes yours by hunting niggers, mostly. Now, if there want no place where they thought they could run to, why they wouldn't run, and you wouldn't be hired to catch 'em.

BEN. All right, Bige. But Tom Gordon's come back, and he swears he'll hunt out Dred, or die.

BIGE. He's a hard un, is Tom Gordon, and so's Dred; we shall see. (*Distant halloos and horn.*)

BEN. Hark, that's the signal, the dogs are on his track again. Come, old fellow, this time we'll have him sure.

(*Exeunt L. Pause. Storm.*)

(*Enter* CIPHER *in a very long skirted old homespun cover coat.*)

CIPHER. Consarn it, any port in a storm; this old coat's better than nothing; it kinder keeps a feller dry. I begin to cipher out prutty smart that I darn't make my stay very long in this Southern country. There's nothing about it, don't hitch with my ideas. No doubt property's property, and all on us humans has, more or less, a kinder hankering arter acquiring on it. But darn it, it somehow seems to me, niggers shouldn't be any body's property, any how; if they be, they're a dreadful skeany property. Now you have 'em, and now you don't have 'em. Here's this old Tiff, now, that Uncle's sent me for the papers about. He should orter belong to himself, have his free papers; and, from his own choice, follow his young mistress, just out of pure love for her and her children. And now it appears, so Uncle makes it out, that he don't belong to himself, but to this Tom Gordon. There's another bad egg—darn my hide, if I wouldn't sooner belong to the old boy than to him. (*Distant shouts, horn and baying of dogs.*) What's that! Shouldn't wonder if that ain't some of them Southern gentlemen, as they say South, trying to recover their property; that is, as we say, hunting down niggers with dogs. (*Noise nearer.*) 'Tis, by thunder; there's them two dogs I see at that fellow's, Ben Dakin's; what, in all creation, are the critturs about!

BEN. (*Outside.*) I see him this way—I can swear to his coat.

CIPHER. Coat! Jehosophat! may bee this is the coat belonged to the nigger they're after—consarn it, they be hunting me down. I'll put for hum, anyhow. (*Music. Runs out. a.. shouts.*) follow, follow; there he goes.

(*Enter* BEN, *running.*)

BEN. There he goes; that's him. Head him off.

BROE. Head him off (*Runs out after* CIPHER.) (*Noise continued.*) CIPHER *returns, coat-tail under his arm.* BEN *after him, full split.*) *Met by* DRED, *with levelled rifle.*

DRED. (*Through music.*) Back, human hell hounds; back, back. (BEN *backs out.* DRED, *with wild laugh.*) For the swamp! for the swamp.

(*Exit after* CIPHER.)

CHANGE OF SCENE.

SCENE V.—*A Front Apartment in the Camena Mansion.*

(*Enter* AUNT MILLY.)

MILLY. I'd gib, pugh, what I hab to gib; I ain't got nothing. But if I had ebber so much, I'd gib it to b'long to Miss Nina, and not her brudder, Tom Gordon. I's so afraid some day he take it into his head to sell me, and dat poor chile, Tom Tit, cas Tom is his'n too. Tom Tit, sister Susan's chile, and sister Susan and me, both belong to Mas'r Tom; dat is, sister Susan did afore she was dead. Heaven rest her soul.

TOM TIT. (*Heard outside singing. Enters, singing some popular nigger air, and dancing to it.*)

MILLY. Hush child, do hush; don't sing and dance now.

TOM. Oh, why not, Aunt Milly! Miss Nina's come back now, and shan't I have good times. I shall tend upon her now, and not poor old missus. De young missus am de missus. (*Sings.*) I bet my money on de bobtail nag.

MILLY. (*Shakes her head, and prays.*)

TOM. Why, aunty, what's the matter with you; what makes you groan so!

MILLY. Laws, dats jist what I used to ask my mother when I was a chile, cause she'd look up at de stars, and keep on groan, groan, groan; and den I used to ax her what makes you groan so.

TOM. And what did she say?

MILLY. She says, matter enough, chile; 'tis thinking of my poor children. I likes to look at the stars, case dey sees the same stars as I do. And then she said, now, child, you may be sold like all my other children, away from your mother; but mind, if you ever gets in any trouble as I does, you mind, chile, you ask God to help you.

TOM. And who is God, Aunt Milly!

MILLY. He is there above us, and can do any thing he likes; and if you are in any kind of trouble, if you ask him, he will help you.

TOM. How must me ask him!

MILLY. Pray to him, my chile, on your two bended knees.

2

TOM. (*Kneels quietly.*) Then, Aunt Milly, I do pray. I pray to him make us all goodness, and can do any thing, if he will please to look down on my Aunt Milly; and whatever her trouble may be, that he will please to lighten her of it. Amen! (*Rises.*) You feel any better now, Aunt Milly!

MILLY. (*Opens her eyes.*) Yes, my child, yes.

TOM TIT. Then, now, I can sing again, if you're out of trouble.

Enter CUFF, *showing in* CLAYTON.

CUFF. Dis way, sar. I hab de honor—

TOM TIT. You have de honor, nigger! No. To introduction de gentlemen am my department. Nigger, have de precidence—quit—make yourself scarce—vanish—abequotulate! (*Waves* CUFF *out,* L. H.)

MILLY. Childe, you is too forward. Allow me, sir.

TOM TIT. (*Puts her aside.*) Aunt Milly, dis ain't in your department, nothers. I is de master of de ceremonies, whar gentlemen is concerned. Dis gentleman hab come to present him to de ladies; and, in course, he has to fix up his twilight.

CLAYTON. I would, if you please, arrange my dressing, which is somewhat disordered by travel, before I present myself.

TOM TIT. Dere, didn't I tell you, Aunt Milly! We men understand dese tings. Aunt Milly, retire. I'll show dis gentleman to his apartment. Make a curtsey, Aunt Milley, and retire.

(AUNT MILLY *makes a short, bobbing curtsey.*)

TOM TIT. You call dat a curtsey, Aunt Milley. Really, I am ashamed of you. Dis am de way. (*Makes a low, ceremonious curtsey. She imitates.*) Dat am better. Retire. (*Both gents laugh.*)

MILLY. Dis childe will be de deff of me. He knows too much, entirely.   (*Exit* R. H., *after curtseying.*)

CLAYTON. And pray, my diminutive little master of the ceremonies, how came you by your knowledge of these matters!

TOM TIT. De Gordons knows every ting. De Gordons am de flower of Old Virginny; Miss Nina am de rose of de family; and I am de tulip.

CLAYTON. (*Laughs.*) Well, lead the way, my little tulip.

TOM TIT. Dis way, sir; dis way. First to de toilet; den to de banquet; den for de ladies. Dat am best of all. (*Bows them out, very ceremoniously.* CLAYTON *bowing and laughing,* R. H.)

CHANGE SCENE.

SCENE VI.—*Handsome apartment, with a gauze window down to the ground, elegantly furnished. Discovered* NINA, AUNT NESBIT, ORTHODOX, UNCLE JOHN. *Lights on side table.* AUNT MILLY *seated on a low stool, at work.*

NINA. Uncle John, now do hush, and let me tell Aunt Nesbit all about it myself.

MRS. NESBIT. I can't believe it. Are you really engaged!

NINA. Yes, to be sure I am—to three gentlemen.

MRS. NESBIT. To three! (*Lifts up her hands and sighs.*) Ah!

ORTHODOX. To three! (*Groans.*)

UNCLE JOHN. (*Aside.*) I'll humor the little puss. (*Aloud.*) To three gentlemen, Nina.

NINA. To three; and I'm going to stay till I find which I like best. May be, you know, Aunt Nesbit, I shan't have any of them.

MRS. NESBIT sighs. ORTHODOX groans.

UNCLE JOHN. But, Nina, do you think that is right?

NINA. Right! Why not? I don't know which to take. I positively don't; so I take them all on trial.

MRS. NESBITT. All on trial!

ORTHODOX. On trial! Oh!

UNCLE JOHN. Perhaps you'll have the goodness to tell us who they are?

NINA. Oh, certainly. Impression No. 1: Mr. Carson, a rich old bachelor, horribly polite; one of those little bobbing men that always have such abiding dickies and collars, and such bright boots, and such tight straps; and he's rich, and perfectly wild about me.

MRS. NESBIT. Perfectly wild!

ORTHODOX. Wild! Oh!

NINA. Stark mad—wouldn't take no for an answer; so I just said yes, to have a little quiet. Besides, he's very convenient about operas, concerts, and such things.

MRS. NESBIT. Operas, concerts, and such things! Ah!

ORTHODOX. And such things. (*Lifts up his hands.*)

UNCLE JOHN. Well; and the next?

NINA. The next is number two—by name, George Emmons. He's one of your pink and white men, who look like cream candy, and, if they were good to eat—

MRS. NESBIT. Pink and white men!

ORTHODOX. Good to eat!

NINA. Yes; he's a lawyer, of good family, thought a great deal of, and all that. Well, really, they say he has talents—I'm no judge. I know he always bores me to death, asking me if I have read this and that—marking places in books, which I never read. He's your sentimental sort—writes the most romantic notes on pink paper, and all that sort of thing.

UNCLE J. (*Aside to her.*) Now, shall I describe the third?

NINA. Now uncle.

UNCLE J. (*Aloud.*) And the third is—

TOM TIT. (*Announcing as he enters,* L. H.) Mr. Edward Clayton, Esq. (*Aside.*) I have been gammoning him closely; he is a gentleman; he is one of us; he'll do; yes, he'll do. (*Steals out* L. W.) I tink we'll have him.

NINA. (*To* UNCLE J.) Oh, uncle John, how could you do so?

UNCLE J. How could I do what, my dear? I assure you I sent for Mr. Clayton to talk on a little matter of business, and to thank him for the interest he has taken in those poor shiftless white trash, the Cripps, and more particularly to their faithful old Tiff.

CLAYTON. Mr. Gordon, I might with much more justice thank you for the benefits you have conferred on those poor wretches; but we

will, if you please, speak of this anon; there are parties here to whom
I am as yet a stranger.

UNCLE J. Oh, I beg pardon. Miss Nina Gordon, permit me. (*Nina
places her hand over his mouth.*) Oh! oh! I forgot, you know Mr.
Clayton, then, Mr. Clayton, permit me to introduce my sister, Mrs.
Nesbit. (MRS. NESBIT *curtseys solemnly.* L. C.) Her spiritual and
ghostly adviser, Mr. Orthodox. (ORTHODOX *bows solemnly.*)

MRS. NESBIT. Mr. Clayton, though I have only now the pleasure of
knowing you, I have heard much of you, and more particularly of
your sister, Miss Anna Clayton. Is it true, pray, that she has a school
for the instruction of the little niggers.

CLAYTON. (C.) She has, madame, and takes particular delight in it.

MRS. NESBIT. (*To* ORTHODOX.) Takes particular delight.

ORTHODOX. In instructing little niggers. Oh!

MRS. NESBIT. One more question, Mr. Clayton, which I trust you
will not think impertinent.

CLAYTON. Oh, madame.

MRS. NESBIT. I have heard—excuse me, sir, if I am wrong—I have
heard, sir, that at the North you have sat in the same pew in church
with a nigger.

CLAYTON. I have, madam, frequently.

MRS. NESBIT. (*To* ORTHODOX.) He has sat in the same pew with a
nigger.

ORTHODOX. With a nigger, frequently. Oh! (*Both groan and retire up.*)

UNCLE J. You observe Mrs. Nesbit is very particular in her religious ideas. You must understand, that when she goes to Heaven
she'll notify them there, forthwith, that she has been accustomed to
the most select circle, and requests to be admitted at the front door.
But now, Nina, come let us take up the subject of our conversation
when Mr. Clayton entered. You must know we have had a full description of two of her intendeds. Come, describe your third.

NINA. Oh, hush! Uncle John.

UNCLE J. Come, come, where's your spirit. I dare you to do it.

NINA. You do; you dare a Gordon; then here goes; No. 3. Well,
his name is Clayton. Mr. Edward Clayton, at your service. (CLAYTON
bows.) He is of your high and mighty people. For his personal appearance I refer you to the—ahem—original picture.

UNCLE J. Not yet in your possession.

NINA. Then, this gentleman is quite different from the other gentlemen. He's kind, but he don't care how he dresses, and sometimes
wears the most horrid shoes; and then he is not polite.

UNCLE J. What?

NINA. Oh, not at all; he won't jump, you know, to pick up your
thread or scissors; and sometimes he'll get into a brown study, and
let you stand ten minutes before he thinks to give you a chair, and all
such provoking things. He isn't a bit of a ladies man. (UNCLE JOHN
and CLAYTON *laugh.* AUNT MILLY *elevating her hands as she sits at
work.* MRS. NESBIT *and* ORTHODOX *groan.*) Well, consequence is, as
my lord wont court the girls, the girls all court my lord.

MRS. NESBIT. Girls all court my lord.

ORTHODOX. Court my lord. Oh!

NINA. Yes, and they seem to think it such a feather in their cap to get attention from him, because you must know he's horrid sensible. So, you see, thats just what set me out to see what I could do with him.

UNCLE J. So you courted him, eh!

NINA. No. indeed, I didn't; but I plagued him, and laughed at him, and spited him, and got him gloriously wroth, and he said some spiteful things about me, and then I said some more about him, and we had a real up and down quarrel; and then I took a penitential turn, you know, and just went gracefullyd own into the valley of humiliation—as we wretches can—and it took wonderfully, brought my lord on his knees before he knew what was the matter. Just then, but he spoke so earnest, and so strong, that he actually got me to crying—hateful creature—and I promised all sorts of things—you know—said altogether more than will bear thinking of.

CLAYTON. But I have thought of all you said deeply, hopefully, and I would—(takes her hand.)

TOM GORDON. (Outside.) Hallo, there! Take my horse, you white nigger, take my horse.

(CLAYTON retires up to back with UNCLE JOHN.)

Enter TOM TIT, L.

TOM TIT. Oh, Miss Nina! here's Mas'r Tom Gordon. Now dere am going to be devil to pay. (Runs over to AUNT MILLY.)

Enter TOM GORDON, L., *drunk—his dress in disorder.*

TOM. I'll make that white nigger, Harry, know who's who. Won't take my horse, won't he—we'll see. Hallo, Nina, is this you! How are you! (Kisses her.)

NINA. Tom, is it you!

TOM. Yes—to be sure. Who did you think it was! Devilish glad to see me, aint you! Suppose you was in hopes I wouldn't come.

NINA. Hush, Tom, do. I am glad to see you. There's a gentleman here—don't speak so loud.

TOM. One of your New-York beaux, eh! I hear you had enough of 'em. Well, I am as good a fellow as any of 'em. Free country, I hope.

NINA. Hush!

TOM. Hush be—hanged. I aint going to whisper for any of 'em. So now, Nina—if there ain't old starchy, to be sure. (Crosses to MRS. NESBIT.) Hallo, old girl! how are you! And you, old praise God barebones. (To ORTHODOX.)

MRS. NESBIT. Thomas! Thomas!

TOM. None of your Thomasing me, you old cat—don't you be telling me to hush. I won't hush, neither. I know what I am about, I guess. It's my house as much it is Nina's; and I am a-going to do as I have a mind to here, and I am going to say what I have a mind to—and in the first place. Nina, you shan't have that fellow, Clayton. He is—

CLAYTON. (Down.) Here to answer for himself. (Distant thunder.)

TOM. Oh, ho! you are here, are you! So much the better—and Uncle John, too—a pretty party of conspirators against my interest; and now I suppose my sister 'll join you too.

CLAYTON. Conspirators—I don't understand.

TOM. Of course you don't. You don't know that that old rascally

nigger, Tiff, (*to* UNCLE JOHN,) that you are harboring on your plantation, belongs to me; and you're aiding and abetting, in harboring my
property from me. He pretends he was left free by his master's will.
No such thing—there's no such will. I bought him, and have the papers to prove it; and I'll have him, if he don't run off to the swamp,
under the protection of the educated outlaw, Dred. And if he does,
I'll hunt him out with dogs, as I have another of my niggers. Ben
Dakin and his dogs shall be on his heels, as they now are on Jim's.

(*Noise outside, of follow! follow! and barking of dogs. CIPHER
rushes over balcony, through c. windows, with only the upper part of
the old overcoat on—all the skirts, up to the armpits, entirely torn off.*)

HARRY. (*Appears at balcony window, speaking.*) Keep back the
dogs. Keep 'em back, or I'll shoot them down.

CIPHER. Shoot 'em, darn 'em; and if you can make a miss, and hit
the fellow that owns 'em, you'll shoot a bigger hound than either of
the dogs.

CLAYTON and UNCLE JOHN. What's the matter!

CIPHER. The matter is, I've been taken for property, and hunted
down with dogs. Look a-here. (*Turns around.*)

TOM. Ha! ha! ha! I see how it is!; he dogs took you for my runaway rascal, Jim. But how's this—how came you with that coat!
That's Jim's coat.

CIPHER. How came I by it! I found it, picked it up and put it on,
in the storm, to keep some papers dry Uncle Judas sent me for.

TOM. Ah! so the dogs took you for him—ha! ha! ha! But come,
let's have the papers.

CIPHER. (*Aside.*) I'll de darned if I'll give 'em to him. He's a nice
article to own human property.

TOM. The papers. The papers.

CIPHER. If you want the papers you must look for tother part of the
coat; your friend, the nigger hunter,'ll give it to you.

TOM. My friend!

CIPHER. Yes, Ben Dakin. Birds of a feather, you know.

TOM. See here. I've heard from your uncle that you are from a red
hot bed of abolitionists, and that you are some of their spawn; and
my opinion is, you've helped my runaway nigger off to the swamp,
and that you have stolen the papers.

CIPHER. See here. I have heard from a good many that you are
one of the blood-thirsty slave owners of the South, that disgrace your
name and country; and my opinion is, if you say I helped off your
nigger to the swamp, that you lie!

TOM. What, you scoundrel! (*Going to strike him with the butt end
of his riding-whip. CIPHER pulls off coat.*)

NINA. Tom! Tom!   (*Interferes. Thunder slow through this.*)

CIPHER. Let him come on. South—slavery against northern liberty.
I'll tan his hide.

TOM. Let me at him, I say. Let go, I say. Nay, then.

(*Hurls away NINA. She would fall, but is caught by HARRY.*)

HARRY. Brute!   (*She nearly faints in his arm.*)

TOM. (*Turns fiercely on him.*) What! you white nigger, dare you
call me brute!

HARRY. I dare! for who but a brute would treat a sister so?

TOM. If you utter another word, I'll whip you within an inch of your life.

HARRY. (*Having released* NINA.) And if you lay a hand upon me, I'le trample you beneath my feet as I would a venemous reptile.

NINA. Harry! Harry! for my sake.

HARRY. My blood is up, and I must speak. The liberty of speech is one of the boasted pillars of your glorious Constitution. Strike me down for using it, as your Senators have done in Washington! Strike me down—trample on me! heap blow on blow! Yet shall my voice be heard ringing in your ears, liberty, liberty! I am a man; the same Heaven is over us—the same power that made us both, now looks down on us. (*Loud thunder.*) And hark, His voice speaks! Now, now! father in Heaven, whilst thou art angry, let thy fiery bolt fall, and strike dead at thy feet he that most belies thine own image. I stand, if not a free man on earth, at least a free man in thy sight. Strike down, if I deserve thy wrath. But let no other hand dare to lay me low.

TOM. Canting hypocrite; Mine shall!

Music. Rushes on HARRY *to strike him.* HARRY *wrests whip from him, and hurls him down—he rises an arm, draws pistol, is about to fire. Thunder bolt strikes behind c. window, with loud crash. Red fire, and* DRED *appears* L. *holding a bleeding negro, his throat all bloody, in his arms.*

DRED. (*Points to* TOM.) The blood of thy slave cries vengeance! And shall have it, I swear!

Women shriek. ORTHODOX, *who has taken up the lights in his hands, drops them.* MRS. NESBIT *faints in a chair.* AUNT MILLY *fans her.* TOM TIT *throws water in her face, &c.*

(PICTURE.)

QUICK DROP.

ACT III.

SCENE I.—*The Dismal Swamp, the retreat of the fugitive slaves; a blasted tree,* c., *up stage, at the foot of which lies the body of the negro* JIM, *his throat torn by the dogs.* DRED *stands on his* L. H., *pointing at the body.* HANNIBAL, JACK, MONDAY, ISAAC, *and other fugitives, male and female, all armed, arranged in a half circle, all in picturesque attitudes, looking and pointing to the body. Drop rises slow to music, and low rumbling of the kettle drums, and occasional thunder. Scene partially dark.*

CHORUS.

The Slave's Oath over the body of a Murdered Brother.

> A Brother's blood! A Brother's blood,
> By cruel white men slain!
> Aloud to Heaven it sends a cry,
> Shall it cry in vain!
>   No, no, we swear,   [*Elevating their rifles.*
>   No, no, we swear,
> Just vengeance we decree;
> Blood for blood shall be our cry,
> We swear on bended knee.   (*Thunder. All kneel.*)

DRED. The oath is registered. (*They rise.*) Brethren, under that tree will be the grave of our brother, adding one more to the list of victims. The destroyer sold his wife—his children—all from him. Therefore he fled—was pursued, the wicked one compassed him round about—the dogs tore him, and licked up his blood—and here will I bury him. Wherefore this place is called "Segar Sahadutha," over the grave of our brethren have ye sworn the oath of vengeance. He that regarded not the oath of brotherhood, let his arm wither and fall from his shoulder blade! Let the arm be broken from the bone! Behold, this curse shall be a witness to you! for it hath heard all the words that ye hath spoken.

(*All murmer deeply.*)

Amen!

DRED. The time approaches, when your arms shall be called upon to strike a blow that shall ring to the confines of the North—a blow for freedom! I await but one more to join us—HARRY—HARRY, of Gordon Plantation—and the hour speeds fast, that shall bring him here for shelter. Even now the scourge of our race, TOM GORDON—the murderer of yon torn and bleeding body, (*points to him,*) seeks his life—aye, worse than life—I see it—as a vision it appears before my eyes—my soul tells me, this bloody monster will seek to tear from Harry's embraces his wife, the wife of his bosom, and sacrifice her to his own vile will. But the avenger will be there! Yes, Dred of the Dismal Swamp will be there! Yes, Dred watches like the panther the steps of that savage wolf, and will yet dye his fangs in his heart's blood. Each man to his post, and as ye hear the yelping of the blood hounds, clutch your weapons; be your hands steady, your aim true. Speed death to the pursuers, freedom to the fugitive slave! Away! Away!

Music. Hurry. All exeunt at different entrances. DRED *threads his way over the Swamp.*

SCENE CLOSES IN, IN 2.

SCENE II.—*Husband and wife. A room in Canema mansion. Door* F. L. H. *Enter, dancing and singing,* TOM TIT, *the negro; air, Root Hog or Die.*

Enter MILLY.

MILLY. Tom Tit, chile, you mustn't go on so. Dar is goin' to be trouble in dis yer house.

TOM TIT. Yes, Aunt Milly, dar must be trouble whar mas'r Tom Gordon is. But you see, Aunt Milly, Miss Nina says, she believes she was born under a dancing star; I believe I was born under two stars at de same time—one dancing, 'tother singing. Can't help my nature, Aunt Milly. (*Sings,*)

"Oh, I'se goin' to glory!
De doo dah, de doo dah."

(*Is dancing out, when he runs against* TOM.)

Enter NINA *and* TOM GORDON.

Tom. Hollo, you noisy young imp ! you, too, are getting too saucy. Take care or I'll sell you—d'ye hear !

Tom Tit. (*Sings very dolefully.*) " Oh, I'se goin' to glory !"

(*Turns round—threatens* Tom *behind his back—*Tom *turns—*Tom Tit *sings again.*)   (*Exit,* Tom Tit.)

Tom. Going to the devil, more likely—like every thing else on the plantation. You want me here to manage the place. Mind, I've told you plainly, you shan't have Clayton ; you shall have that other chap —Carson. He has one of the largest properties in New York. Joe Snieder has told me about him.

Nina. I shall *not* have him, say what you please ; and I *shall* have Mr. Clayton, if I choose. You have no right to dictate to me of my own affairs ; and I shan't submit to it—I tell you frankly.

Tom. Highty-tighty ! We are coming up, to be sure.

Nina. Moreover, I wish you to understand, I'll have no more such scenes enacted under this roof as took place last night—had you been yourself, I scarcely think my father's son would have so behaved.

Tom. (*Sneeringly.*) Myself ! Oh, I was drunk, was I ! Of course I was.

Nina. No matter ; I wish you to let everything in this place entirely alone ; and remember that my servants are not your servants, and that you have no control over them, whatever.

Tom. We'll soon see how you'll help yourself. I am not going skulking about my father's place as if I had no right or title there. You shall shortly find I have as good a right and title—aye, and per- haps a better than yourself, to give my orders here ; and if your nig- gers don't look sharp, they'll find out whether I am master here or not—especially that Harry. If the dog dare only to look ugly at me, or to countermand any of my orders, I'd put a bullet through his head, as soon as I would through a buck's. I give you warning !

(Milly, *at back, lifts her hand.*)

(*Exit,* Tom.)

Milly. Miss Nina, honey, can't you make some errand to get Harry off de place, while Mas'r Tom's round !

Nina. By what right has he to dictate to my servants, or to me ; or to interfere with any of my arrangements here !

Milly. Oh, dere's no use talkin' about rights, honey ; we must all do what we ken. Don't make much odds whether our rights is one way or 'tother. You see, chile, its just here—Harry's you're right hand ; but you see he hain't learnt to *ben* before de wind, like de rest of us. He is mighty spirity ; he is just as full now as a powder-keg ; and Mas'r Tom is bent on aggravatin' him—and laws, chile, dere may be bloody work—dar may so !

Nina. Why, do you think he'd dare !

Milly. Chile, don't talk to me. Dare ! yes, sure enouff he will dare. Didn't you see last night ! Besides, dere's fifty ways young gentlemen may take to aggravate and provoke ; and when flesh and blood can't stand it no longer, Harry will raise his hand, and den shoot him down ! Nothing said—nothing done. You won't want to have a lawsuit with your own brother ! And if you did, it wouldn't bring

2*

Harry to life. Laws, chile, if I could tell you what I've seen—you don't know nothing about it. Now, I tell you, get up some message to your uncle's plantation, send him off for anything—for nothing—only have him gone ; and then speak to Mas'r Tom fair, and may be he'll go off. But don't quarrel, don't cross him—come what may. Dar ain't a soul on de place can bear de sight of him. But den you see de rest dey *all friends*, Harry won't bend ; so, chile, you must be quick about it.

(HARRY *speaks outside*.)

HARRY. Have my horse led round by the fruit walk.

Enter HARRY ; MILLY *goes up*.

MILLY. Harry, try to bend for once.

3 NINA. Harry, I am glad you are here, and have your horse ready. I want you to go over to Uncle John's plantation, and carry a note for me.

(HARRY *bends his eyes on the ground, and folds his arms*.)

NINA. And, Harry, I think you had better make some business o' errand to keep you away two or three days, or a week.

HARRY. Miss Nina, this is seed time ; the business is pressing, and very particular, and needs my constant overlooking. A few days neglect, now, may produce a great loss, and then it will be said, I neglected my business to idle and ride round the country.

NINA. Well, but if I send you, I take the responsibility, and I bear the loss. The fact is, I am afraid, Harry, you won't have patience to be here now Tom's at home. In fact, Harry, I'm afraid of your life.

HARRY. Isn't this outrageous—beyond human endurance ? that everything must be left to ruin, and all because I havn't the right to stand up like a man, and protect you and yours.

NINA. It is a pity, it is a shame. But Harry, don't stop to think upon it ; go, go. (*Lays her hand on his shoulder*.) For my sake, be good, be good.

(TOM GORDON *outside*, L. H.) 'Pon my soul, you're a pretty little concern.

HARRY. Look there, Miss Nina, do you see my wife and your brother. (*Goes up ; Nina restraining*.)

Enter LISSETTE, *with a bouquet, followed by* TOM GORDON, L. H.

TOM. Wither go you, my pretty one, eh ?

LISSETTE. To Miss Nina Gordon, sir.

TOM. Ay, and pray who do you belong to, my pretty little puss ? I think I have never seen you on this place.

LISSETTE. Please, sir, I am Harry's wife.

TOM. (*In thought for a moment*.) Indeed, you are, eh ? Harry's wife, Harry's wife ; hum ! (LISSETTE *is going*.) Stay, stay. (*Lays his hand on her shoulder ;* NINA *restrains* HARRY.) Dev'lish good taste that nigger Harry has.

LISSETTE. Nigger, sir !

TOM. Ay, don't you know, my pretty, that I am your husband's young master, (LISSETTE *shrinks from him*) and I mus—

NINA *advances before Harry can get down*.

NINA. Tom Gordon, I am ashamed of you. Silence, sir; silence! (*Stamps her foot.*) Dare to come to my place and take such liberties here. You shall not be allowed, sir, while I *am* mistress. Dare to lay a finger on this girl while she is under my protection! Come, Lissette, (HARRY *comes down,* R., *and takes* LISSETTE, *to a husband's arms.* NINA *clasps her hands.*)

NINA. Oh, Harry! brother!

LISSETTE. Husband.

HARRY. Fear not. (*The brothers regard each other.*)

TOM. (*Lifts his hat ironically.*) 'Pon my word, Mister Harry, we are all under the greatest obligations to you for bringing such a pretty little fancy article here.

HARRY. My wife does not belong to this place. She belongs to Mrs. Le Clerc, of the Belle Vue plantation.

TOM. Ah, thank you for the information. I have been wanting a pretty concern of that sort. She's a good housekeeper, isn't she? does up shirts well? what do you suppose she could be bought for? I will go and see her mistress.

During this, HARRY *advances a little, as if about to give way to his passion; then suddenly folds his arms, compresses his lips, directs his eyes to the two women clinging to each other. A pause.* TOM *turns on his heel.*

TOM. For Belle Vue plantation   (*Exit* L. H., *whistling.*)

NINA. Harry!

LISSETTE. Husband!

HARRY. (*Bursts into a bitter laugh.*) Husband! Ha, ha, ha! Don't you hear, you may be *bought* from me.

LISSETTE. Never; I will die first!

NINA. She shall not; I'll send and buy her myself.

HARRY. You don't know how your affairs stand; you haven't the money; he may have a thousand dollars! Great Heaven! havn't I borne this yoke long enough. (*Covers his face.*)

NINA. Harry, Harry! I'll sell all I have; jewels, everything. I'll mortgage the estate before Tom Gordon shall do this thing. I am not quite so selfish as I have always seemed to be. You have sacrificed all for me. I have as much energy as any Gordon of them all, when I am roused. (*Calls.*) Here Tom Tit! (*Enter* TOM.) Tom Tit, tell Aunt Milly Lissette is under her charge; then fly over to Mr. Clayton, say I would see him instantly.

TOM TIT. With the utmost felicity, both orders shall be obeyed. The protection ob de fair sex am my greatest delight: and my next is, de communication wid a real gentleman. (*Looks at* HARRY, *then turns to* LISSETTE.) Will you honor me with the tips of your delicate fingers? (*Leads her out,* L. H.)

NINA. Now, Harry, you must keep out of the way; you must obey me.

HARRY. (*With feeling.*) Miss Nina, dear Miss Nina, I could serve you to the last drop of my blood! But (*in a severe tone*) I hate, yes, I detest everybody else; yes, I hate your color, I hate your country, your laws.

NINA. Harry! you do wrong. You forget yourself.

HARRY. Oh! I do wrong, do I! We are the people that are never to do wrong. People may stick pins in us, and stick knives in us, wipe their shoes on us, spit in our face, we must be amiable, we must be models of Christian patience! I tell you your father should rather have put me into quarters, made me work like a common negro in the field, than have given me the education he did, and leave me under the foot of every white man that dares tread on me. (*Crosses.*)

NINA. (*Aside.*) Strange! How like my father he looks, in that fearful burst of passion! Harry, Harry! if you love me be quiet!

HARRY. (*Softened instantly.*) Love you! You have always held my heart in your hand! That, and that only, has been the lock upon chain. If it had not been for you—for the dear love I bear you—I should have fought my way to to the North long before now, or I would have at least found a grave upon the road. (*Crosses.*)

NINA. (*After a moment of thought.*) Harry, my love shall no longer be a lock upon your chain; for, as there is a Heaven above us, I will set you free! Now, Harry, go!

HARRY. (*Kisses her hand.*) God bless you! God bless you!

Enter TOM TIT, L.

TOM TIT. Miss Nina, Mr. Clayton am in de drawing-room.

NINA. I fly to him, Harry! Your wife shall be free—she shall be yours, and yours only. (*Exit*, L.)

HARRY.—Yes, I believe her; she will keep her word. Lisette will be free! She will be mine, mine! Am I not a slave? A slave can own nothing. But, hold! Miss Nina will marry Mr. Clayton. She will no longer need my money. Yes, I can, without injuring her, purchase my own freedom. Let me not delay! The money! The money!   (*Exit*, L. H.)

SCENE III.—*The forged will—front chamber in Canema.*

Enter CIPHER CUTE, *disguised in overcoat and slouched hat, and heavy whip—belt under overcoat, with two very long pistols in it.*

CIPHER. Guess I look considerable like a law student, in a horn. I come to study law under Uncle Judas; but I've giu up, and took tew t'other side justice. I dew think Uncle Judas is about as big a scoundrel as there is out. But I musn't lose time. If I could see any body, now, tew show me tew the young lady. (*Looking* R.) Hollo! I say, you black bird, say!

Enter TOM TIT, R. H.

Look a-here, my little boy; show me to Miss Nina.

Tom eyes him from head to foot with supreme contempt.

TOM TIT. Boy! Where do you get your men, I should like to know! Miss Nina am busy wid a *gentleman.* She haint no time to trow away upon such as you.

CIPHER. (*Whistles.*) Dem it! What a long tail our cat has got, to be sure. Guess she'll see sich as me, if you'll tell her there's life and death hangs on what I have tew say.

Tom Tit. I can't carry messages for common people. You can write it down, and I'll carry it to Miss Nina on a waity.

Cipher. O git eout! I'll go tew her myself. (*Going* r.)

Tom Tit. Stand back! We command!

Cipher. We! we! we! See here: if you don't stand out of my way, I'll open my mouth, make one gulp, and swallow you whole, without grease.

Enter Nina *and* Clayton, r. h.

Cipher. Oh, here you be! This giant-killer, here, wouldn't let me come to you.

Tom Tit. He wanted to intrude—

Cipher. O shut up, grasshopper!

Tom Tit. White trash! (*Exit*, r., *with*.)

Cipher. Excuse me, miss—and yet no time for ceremony—I'm mighty glad I have found both of tew once. For though you are not man and wife, yet, still, as you soon must be—

Nina. Sir!

Cipher. As you can't no longer be without a protector, now your brother Tom's come out in his true colors.

Nina. Your meaning, sir?

Cipher. Is this: Uncle Jekyl's Tom Gordon's man of law. I'm Uncle Jekyl's clerk. I've overheard a plot, that Tom Gordon's coming down on you with a false will of your father's. Here's a copy I made. (*Hands it to* Clayton.) And will prove the original will of Colonel Gordon's to be a forgery.

Clayton. By Heaven! its true. Here's a will leaving all the estates to Tom Gordon.

Nina. Good Heavens! What's to be done!

Cipher. I'll tell you: Go you, both, over to Uncle John Gordon's; show him that forgery; get his advice; and then you (*to* Clayton) hurry back to Magnolia Grove. There's mischief brewing for you tew.

Clayton. What mischief!

Cipher. Be ready for the worst that Tom Gordon can do you. I heard him threaten to burn down your nigger school-house; and if you interfered, look out for your life. He's a man of action. No time must be lost. I am a man of action; and as he's only *law* to back him, and I have justice on my side, we'll see who'll come out at the right end of the horn. Now dew as I say, and quick. I'm off tew old Tiff. That poor, old, faithful critter shan't want justice while I can deal it out. Uncle Judas says I'm a fool, and shall never be worth a cent. May be so. I may go back home with my pockets empty; but if my heart is full of the knowledge that I have defended the innocent, and succored the oppressed, I shall go home happy. I shall, by Jehosophet!

(*Exit*, l. h.)

Nina. Clayton, all reserve must give way under present circumstances. I am indeed in need of a protector. I fear my brother; I know him to be violent and revengeful. Should he get this estate but for a day, deeds of blood, deeds shocking to think of, would be done. Lissette's honor—Harry's life would not be a moment safe. Give me your protection—your advice—your aid, to prevent so dreadful a catastrophe.

CLAYTON. My services, my life are at your disposal.

NINA. I accept, and will repay them.

CLAYTON. With yourself?

NINA. I will! (*Giving hand.*)

CLAYTON. (*Kissing her hand.*) Then have I a husband's right! And now, first to leave Lissette under my sister's care; and then to your uncle, where I will leave you, and return to Magnolia Grove to protect from violence—

NINA. No, no—I will not leave you. If any violence threaten you, it threatens me. Let come what will, by your side I can face it fearlessly.

CLAYTON. Be it so! Come, then, not a moment must be lost.

(*Exit, R. H.*)

SCENE IV.—*The faithful slave. Escape to the swamp. Interior of* CRIPPS' *cabin, as before.* MUSIC. *Picture:* MRS. CRIPPS *lying on the floor, c., on each side of her, one of her children kneeling—*OLD TIFF *supporting her head.*

TIFF. Honey, darling, remember this yer one tex what de minister preached at de last camp-meeting. He say, (*solemnly,*) "Come unto me, all ye who labor and are heavy laden, and I will give you rest." (*Wipes her eye with his cuff.*)

MRS. C. Rest, rest, rest. Oh, how much I want it! Did he say that was in the Bible?

TIFF. Yes, he said so; and I spects, by all he said, it's de word from dar—'tis His voice what says it—(*points up.*) It always makes me feel much better to think on it. It 'peared like it was just what I was wanting to hear.

MRS. C. And I too, Tiff—Tiff, hark! (*Pause.*) I hear a voice now—yes, it says those very words—"Come out to me, all ye who labor and are heavy laden, and I will give you rest." Tiff, I'm going to rest; I see—I see the One Who says that; and its all true —Tiff—its growing dark—where are my children? (*They place their hands in their mother's.*) I can only feel them—God bless my children. Tiff, to you—I leave them—God bless—rest—rest—rest.

(*MUSIC. She dies—*TIFF *bends over her, and sobs.*)

TIFF. She am gone! Dead, dead, dead; but she am, I hope, in a better place—Heaven. Heaven be her rest! Yes, poor, dear honey love, Tiff will take care of de children; he will nebber, nebber leave them, nebber! de grave alone shall hide him from dem. De grave alone—yes, only de grave shall part us. Heaven hears old Tiff promise.

CRIPPS. (*Outside.*) Come in, boys; There's a drop in the demijohn yet.

TIFF. His wife lying here a corpse, and he drunk!

Enter CRIPPS, BEN DAKIN, BIGE SKINFLINT, *and* CIPHER *disguised.*

TIFF. (*Rises and points to the body.*) Dar, dar, you wouldn't believe her last night! Now what you tink ob dat ar! See how you look now. Good Shepherd hear you abusing de poor lamb, and he's took her whar you'll nebber see her again.

CRIPPS. What, dead!   Who'd have thought it!

(Staggers to bed, and sits on it.)

TIFF. Ah, who!   Get up dar, and let me lay de poor lamb down decent.

CRIPPS. No, no, not here; I'm going to sleep myself.

(Very drunk—falls back on bed.)

BEN. See here, Bige, lend a hand to move the body.

TIFF. Not one dar to lay a finger on my poor lamb.

BEN. Then move her yourself, and come back right away; I have business for you.

TIFF. *(Lifts up the body.)* Dar, poor lamb, I'll lay you in Miss Fanny's bed; and you, children, come wid me.

(Bears her out, R. Q. E., followed by children.)

CIPHER. This is a pretty picture of human natur—but I must keep dark.

(BEN and BIGE seat themselves at table, on which is a large demijohn and one tin cup, during the time TIFF carries out the body.)

BEN. Why in thunder didn't this drunken fool tell us there was death in the house.

BIGE. He can't help it; besides, business is business.

CIPHER. *(Aside.)* Guess Belzebub will have his hands full when he puts his claws on you two.

BEN. Come, take a drink.   *(Pours out, and drinks—hands cup and demijohn to Dije, who does the same.)* Now, then, to business. Stranger, you say you want a good cook.

CIPHER. I dew.

BEN. Then I have the very lot that will suit you without going further.   Here, you, Tiff, come in here.

Enter TIFF, wiping his eyes with a very ragged old pocket handkerchief.

BEN. There, that's the dientical article; there's not a better cook in all North Caroliny.   And you shall have him for eight hundred dollars—dog cheap!

CIPHER. *Dog* cheap!   I should think it was.

TIFF. *(Looks on with wonder.)* You don't mean me, mas'r!

BEN. I don't mean anything else.

TIFF. What!   Sell me!

BEN. Aye, on account of your master, Mr. Tom Gordon.

TIFF. *(In utter astonishment.)* What am dis!   Am I awake!   De laws!   He dar, *(points to bed,)* last night, said something 'bout dis. But, mas'r Ben Dakin, I hab my free papers here, here in dis trunk.

(Opens it—starts back with horror!)

Gone!

BEN. Gone.   Ha!   Ha!   What never was there.

TIFF. As I hope for Heaven—

BEN. Oh, come, none of your preaching.   *(Rises.)* Here, here's the first present your master makes you—a pair of bracelets.

(Puts handcuffs on TIFF.   During this, SKINFLINT drinks once or twice, getting sleepy—drunk.   Stage darkens by degrees.)

CIPHER. *(Aside.)* Dern your hide, if I have a chance I'll yut iron bracelets on to you red hot.

TIFF. But de children, mas'r—de poor children dat I promise to pertect!

BEN. (*On table.*) Oh, they'll be taken care of. I don't know what Tom Gordon wants to do with 'em, but he told me to take charge on 'em—particularly the gal. Hello, Bige! What! sowed up!

BIGE. Hic! Sowed up, yourself—I—I—an't drunk. I'm on'y overcome. I—I—Hic!—can't a bear the sight of a corpse!—Where's the whiskey!

(*Feels for the demijohn, and would upset it; but* BEN *prevents it.* BIGE *utters an exclamation, and falls from his chair—which is near the door—laying across the entrance.*)

BEN. Drunken fool! lie there; that's all you're good for. Come, stranger, let's drink. I'm waiting here for that old nigger's master. He's one of the real blood—he's no gammon about him; knows the ace of spades from the king of diamonds. He's a true Southerner—he is.

CIPHER. Consarn the critter! If he don't get drunk soon, and hold his cussed jaws, I shall have to cut his throat. See here, stranger, I'll buy that nigger, and give you my note for him.

BEN. Your *note!* And who are you, any how! Where from—North or South!

CIPHER. Well, North, I guess.

BEN. I thought so. Its only such trash talks about giving notes.

CIPHER. Who do you call trash!

BEN. You, and every cussed Yankee like you. (*Rises.*) I suppose you come to get this nigger to let him free—eh! I'd rather put this into him first. (*Draws a long bowie knife.*) D'ye see that!

CIPHER. (*Cooly rises—goes close up to the knife—brings his eye down to the handle, and then lets it travel up to the point slowly.*) I dew!

BEN. That's what I call a particeler Southern argument agin Northern abolition.

CIPHER. Shouldn't wonder. Heow long will such an argument reach!

BEN. About arm's length—its mighty cutting. (*Stretches out his arm.*)

CIPHER. Jest so. (*Deliberately draws a very long pistol from his inside belt, and levels it at* BEN.) And this is a popping rejoinder. 'Tis but fair tew meet men with their own arguments.

BEN. (*Laughs in a drunken way.*) All right. That's a fact. I like you, stranger. Come, sit down. (*They sit.*) Let's take a drink. (*Pours out liquor—hands it to* CIPHER.)

CIPHER. (*Looks in cup.*) Look a here—d'ye call that a horn! Why it ain't half a one—no sneaking drinks for me. (*Takes demijohn—pretends to pour it.*) There—a full cup or none. (*Drinks it all.*) Drink like a man.

BEN. (*Admiringly.*) You're a man, any how—so am I. I never see the man yet that could floor me. Give us hold. (*Takes demijohn—fills a bumper, till it runs over.*) Is that a horn! Here she goes. (*Drinks it.*) And now, stranger, (*taking out a pack of cards,*) I'll play a game of poker with you for a nigger. (*Very drunk.*) I'll go you blind for a nigger. Hurrah! And if I lose my nigger, I'll stake my best dogs—the best dogs for pulling down a nig—nig—ger in—the—country.

(*Falls forward on the table, and sleeps. By this time stage quite dark, and old* TIFF *has sat down on a low stool,* R., *near 2d* E., *and is rocking himself back and forwards.* MUSIC, P.P., *cautious.*)

CYPHER. Here, old man, not a word; I'm your friend; there, there (*gives papers*) are your free papers—never mind how I got 'em; don't speak. They wouldn't be of no use to you if Tom Gordon got hold of you; but he shan't. Hold on! your hands must be free. (*Goes to* BEN *and takes a bunch of keys from his belt, unlocks handcuffs.*) But first call out your children.

TIFF goes to door, R. Q. E. Children Enter.

CIPHER. (*To* TEDDY.) See here, be you man enough to hold this! (*Gives him a pistol, and places him on table close to* BEN.) There. now, if you see that big ugly head only move, you pull that little thing under there, that's all. (*Places muzzle of pistol to* BEN*'s head.*) Now, old Tiff, you must off to the swamp with these children.

TIFF. But her, my poor mistress, who shall bury her!

CIPHER. Hush, you shall, or I will, only get away now. (*Goes to window in flat, opens it, places stool under it, gets* TIFF *out first, then hands out the children, the boy. As he gets out himself the stool falls,* BEN *starts up.*)

BEN. Hollo! escaped! up, up, here! (*Runs to window, the shutter, which is a wooden one, is shut in his face*)

BIGE. (*Rises*) The door, the door! after them! call my dogs! (*They're rushing to door—it opens—*DRED *appears with levelled gun.*)

SCENE CLOSES

SCENE V.—*Front Wood.* TOM *and* JEKYL *outside.*

JEKYL. But, Mr. Gordon, sir, but sir!

TOM. (*As he enters collaring* JEKYL.) But, scoundrel, what are you for if you can't keep what I give you in charge, (*Shakes him.*)

JEKYL. My nephew, my nephew, Mr. Gordon, he stole the papers, 'twant my fault.

TOM. (*Throws him off.*) Curse you and your nephew too. What's to be done!

JEKYL. If I might advise.

TOM. I have it. I'll brazen it out. Did you warn Stokes and Athen, and the rest, to meet me here?

JEKYL. I did; and they are here now.

TOM. Then damn the apers! my will's law enough—we' ll do without 'em.

Enter JIM STOKES *and* BILL.

JIM. Here we are, squire.

TOM. Where's Bob Story, Jim Dexter and the rest of the crow.

JIM. They'll meet us at the spot.

TOM. All right; and you're all determined to stand by and aid me in taking my own, and to give that abolitionist, Clayton, a lesson he won't forget,

JIM and BILL. Ay, we'll do it, we'll stand by you.

TOM. And you (*to* JEKYL,) bring me your nephew with my papers, or curse me if you shan't take his place, and I'll throw your pettifogging carcass into the flames, instead of his. (*Enter hurriedly* BEN DAKIN *and* BIGE SLINKINL.) Now then, where's my old nigger, Tiff, and those children?

BEN. Off to the swamp, squire; run away.

TOM. And you, you scoundrel!

BEN. Hold on, hold on, squire; I come here to do you a service. If you go on so I shall do you a mischief, by thunder I shall.

TOM. Every thing thwarts me and drives me mad. Never mind, I'll have my revenge one way. Yes, that shall not be denied me. I'll have the plantation yet. I'll carry off my own slave, Lissette, and shoot down Harry, and burn down Clayton's abolition den over his head. You're all sworn to assist me, boys.

ALL. All! All!

TOM. Then to work! follow me!

Hurry Exeunt.

THE BROTHERS—SLAVE AND FREE.

SCENE VI.—*Exterior of* CLAYTON's *house at Magnolia Grove. Flats in three first cut wood wings. Door practicable flat. Enter from D. F.* LISSETTE *with banjo to symphony of her song. Song.*

"What are the joys of white man here."

I sing that song because it is Harry's favorite; but my heart does not respond to it as it used in our own little home. But 'tis only for a day, and then I shall return more happy than ever, for Mr. Clayton says I shall be a free woman. Oh, and Harry too, he will soon be his own master. Then I shouldn't wonder if he takes me to see the world, even all the way to New-York.

TOM *Enters*, U. E. R. *during this, with* BEN DAKIN *and others; motions them off.*

TOM. (*Puts arm round her.*) He won't, but I will.

LISSETTE. (*Screams.*) Ah!

TOM. Hush, you fool!

LISSETTE. I won't—I hate you; help! help!

TOM. I'll throttle you if you don't keep silent.

(*Going towards her. Enter* NINA, D. F. *followed by* CLAYTON *and* UNCLE JOHN.)

NINA. What outrage is this?

TOM. Outrage! 'tis none. I claim my property—this girl is mine, I have purchased and paid for her, and I now claim her.

NINA. Shame upon you; I will not call you brother; you are a disgrace to the name of Gordon. This you do out of revenge. But you will not tear this poor girl from her home, from her husband. You will not be so inhuman!

TOM. Inhuman! Show a drowning wretch a spar, and tell him not to clutch it. I tell you, as easily as he at his last gasp would refrain, so would I now from holding fast to that girl. Not drag her from her husband! That is my joy; ay, my joy.

UNCLE JOHN. But, Tom, Tom, listen to reason!

TOM. To none that you can urge—are you going to join against me too! Have I not a right to take my own!

UNCLE JOHN. True, but—but—damn it, Tom, if you take that girl only out of motives of revenge, you are no longer a nephew of mine. I disclaim you!

TOM. Ha! ha! ha!

CLAYTON. If no other motive will move you, perhaps interest will. I will double, nay, treble the price you gave for her, so you will let her remain with her husband.

TOM. Not for ten times the sum—keep your breath to defend your own cause, you may shortly need it I repeat, this girl is my slave—I claim her; she shall go with me now. If she refuses, I will manacle her, and have her whipt—prevent me, any one, at your own proper peril. Thus I seize!

(HARRY *rushes in from* R. Q. E. *between* LISETTE *and* TOM.)

HARRY. And if you do, it must be over my lifeless body.

TOM. (*Coolly.*) Eh! No! I expected this. Your death at present is not my aim. Hark ye, sirrah, you too are my slave!

HARRY. I!

UNCLE JOHN and MINA. How! your slave!

TOM. (*Aside.*) 'Tis only the copy of the will, if any, they have seen. I'll brazen it out. (*To* UNCLE JOHN.) You ask how; then you will I answer: the Canema Plantation is mine; I have my father's will to prove it. The will, by virtue of which that girl (*points to* NINA) held it, is a forgery.

NINA. O Heavens! the villany!

TOM. I'm prepared to prove it.

HARRY. But I have purchased myself, this day, this hour. I call upon—upon men to witness—here—here—is the paper given by Colonel Gordon, granting me my freedom upon payment of a certain sum; witnessed by Mr. John Gordon—then that sum I have paid this day, and I am free.

NINA. He has, he is free!

TOM. He is not. He is my slave. Mr. Gordon knows, you all know, a slave not being a person in the eye of the law, cannot have a contract made with him! That paper is worthless, you are a slave, (*to* HARRY,) my slave!

HARRY. In death, perhaps—never in life your slave! Great Heaven! For twenty years have I kept the hope of freedom nearest my heart—and now to have it torn thus cruelly away!

CLAYTON. This injustice must not, shall not be!

TOM. I told you to look to your own affairs. What Ho's there! Fire that nest of abolitionism, that nigger school-house, and burn it to the ground.

(*Shouts,* U. E. L., *and torches seen to flash.*)

HARRY. Oh, villian! villian!

TOM. Oh, Slave! slave!

HARRY. Slave! Carry us to the wilderness—place us man to man! No eye to see—no hand to help, and let us grapple! Then the poor

slave's natural strength 'gainst the proud white man's power. Slave
as I am, we are one common stock—not only from there, (*points to
Heaven,*) but by blood, by the nearest ties—your father was mine!
Yes, Colonel Gordon was my father! I am your brother—your elder
brother! Now let nature's just laws prevail! I am the eldest son!
I ought to claim my rights! Which of us has been a brother to you
trembling maid! (*Points to* NINA, *who clings to* CLAYTON, L. H.).You
or I! Well, let that pass. She's your sister, not the poor slave's.
But here, here is *my wife*. She is mine in the eyes of Heaven, and by
Heaven I will have her. Lissette, cling to me. Clasp me firmly;
these slave arms shall defend you, and bear you to the swamp and
freedom! Way there, way!

> *Music. Lifts up* LISSETTE *and rushes out with her,* R. Q. E. TOM
> *rushes after him, when* CIPHER *appears with long gun—points it at
> him. Picture. Shouts,* U. E. L. *Red fire! Large Bell! Negroes
> rush hurriedly in, all crying fire! Stage quite dark. Close in one.*

   "FLIGHT AND PURSUIT."   "BROTHER AFTER BROTHER."

SCENE VII.—*Wood—dark. Hurried music—shouts—bell is heard.
        Enter* HARRY, *bearing* LISSETTE, *led by* DRED.

DRED. Away! away! I will follow! To the swamp! to the
swamp! freedom awaits you there!   (*Exeunt* L. H.)

            Enter TOM, DAKIN *and* SKINFLINT, R. H.

TOM. Five thousand dollars for Harry, dead or alive. Show me
his blood—I must, I will have it. Call all the fellows—leave Clayton alone for the present. We'll hunt Harry and that psalm-singing
villain, Dred, to the death! They or I, by Heaven, live not another
night! Set on the dogs! raise the hue and cry! Come on! come
on!
ALL. (*Rush out, shouting.*) "Death to the runaway!"

                         RETRIBUTION.

SCENE VIII.—*Swamp by moonlight.* DRED *on the path, leading in
   HARRY and* LISSETTE; OLD TIFF *and the children, looking towards
   them as they reach the stage;* TOM *is seen on the path.* TOM *fires at*
   DRED; DRED *staggers—recovers himself—fires his gun;* TOM, *with a
   wild cry, elevates his arm, and falls back into the swamp.*

DRED. (*Staggers—falls, centre.*) Harry, I meant to use you in
deeds of blood, to set the black man free; but 'tis not so decreed—
other means must work out Heaven's will. Blood has been shed
enough—shed no more—your greatest enemy is removed. Be patient, if made to suffer; Heaven will, in its own good time, set all
free.
(DRED *dies. Slow music.* HARRY *and* LISSETTE *kneel on side,* C. L.;
TIFF *and children,* R. H. *Blue fire. Picture.*)
                                           (DROP FALLS.)

                    END OF ACT THIRD.

ACT IV.

SCENE FIRST AND LAST.—*Morning breaks—freedom and happiness. A handsome garden, with balustrade across platform behind; with curtain to draw up to show tableau and transparency; garden seats ranged R. H.* UNCLE JOHN *and* MRS. GORDON *heard outside,* R.

UNCLE JOHN. Mrs. G., Mrs. G., I will have my own way.
MRS. GORDON. No you wont.

They enter. UNCLE JOHN *dressed as for a wedding, a Bouquet and white favor in his coat.*

UNCLE JOHN. I say I will.
MRS. GORDON. And I say you wont.
UNCLE JOHN. D——hang it! Mrs. G., don't I know my own mind!
MRS. GORDON. No!
UNCLE JOHN. I say I do; and I wont give my consent to Nina's marrying Clayton.
MRS. GORDON. Yes you will. If you didn't mean to do so, why that dress! Why are you here, at Magnolia Grove!
UNCLE JOHN. Why—why I came to refuse my consent, and command Nina not to have Clayton, without he promises to give up his absurd plan of educating his niggers. It wont do—it will be the ruin of 'em all; and I must put a stop to it.
MRS. GORDON. You, fudge.
UNCLE JOHN. Fudge, Mrs. G.
MRS. GORDON. Yes, Mr. J., fudge.
UNCLE JOHN. What do you mean by fudge! Mrs. G.
MRS. GORDON. You'll see. Here comes Nina and Clayton, they'll be my answer.

Enter NINA, *in a wedding dress,* and CLAYTON, R. Q. E, *followed by* MILLY.

NINA. (*Runs to* UNCLE JOHN.) My dear uncle, your consent and blessing.
UNCLE JOHN. I won't give it.
MRS. GORDON. He don't mean it.
UNCLE JOHN. I do. Clayton must first abandon his plan of educating his niggers. It's all humbug.
NINA. Humbug, uncle, say not so. Here comes an apt illustration to the contrary. (*Enter* HARRY, *dressed, and* LISSETTE. R. Q. E.) Where would have been my plantation! ruined, and myself a beggar, had it not been for Harry; and education fitted Harry for my manager.
HARRY. 'Tis true, sir, and I am satisfied education, properly directed, will fit us all, not only to be good managers for others, but will do that which is of still more infinite importance, teach us how to manage ourselves.

Enter MRS. NESBIT *and* ORTHODOX.

UNCLE JOHN. Very good—capital. Confess, now, Clayton—confess that was not all Dulcimer's work.

TOM TIT. (*Advances, c.*) Both words and music—by de author. (*Bows.*)

(ALL.) What!—Tom Tit!

TOM TIT. (*Bows.*) I have de honor.

(*Here he can be called on to sing, if thought proper by* UNCLE JOHN. *Then dancing by the minstrels and* TOM TIT *after all is done.*)

HARRY. As Miss Nina's happiness—

NINA. Say your sister, Harry.

(HARRY *takes her hand.*)

HARRY. As my sister's happiness has always been my first care and fondest desire, I am anxious that no cloud should mar it at this moment, and as Mr. John Gordon—

UNCLE JOHN. Say uncle, Harry.

HARRY. As Uncle John Gordon's prejudices against education remain in a measure unanswered, I have prepared a little scene by which they may possibly be overcome—when he will consent to, and bless my sister's union.

TOM TIT *waives his baton—all stand aside—when he waives it up at the curtain at back—which draws entirely up, disclosing*

GRAND TABLEAUX,

Transparency, Lettered

" EDUCATION "

" LEADS TO PRESENT AMELIORATION "

" AND ULTIMATE "

"LIBERTY."

School Children. } FIGURE of GODDESS OF LIBERTY, on *Pedestal.* c. { *School Children.*

(UNCLE JOHN *joins* CLAYTON's *and* NINA's *hands.*)

HARRY. Education leads to present amelioration, and ultimate liberty. When education is fully carried into effect, we shall need no more Dreds to protect fugitive slaves—nor read more tales of the *great Dismal Swamp.*

MUSIC.

Chorus of children at back, as in 2d Act, as

CURTAIN DESCENDS.

FRENCH'S
AMERICAN DRAMA.
NO. 78.

OUR JEMIMY;

OR.

CONNECTICUT COURTSHIP,

A

FARCE IN ONE ACT,

WRITTEN FOR

MRS. BARNEY WILLIAMS.

With Cast of Characters, Stage Business, Costumes, Relative Positions, &c. &c.

AS NOW PERFORMED AT THE PRINCIPAL THEATRES
IN THE UNITED STATES.

NEW-YORK:
SAMUEL FRENCH,
121 NASSAU-STREET.

PRICE,   12½ CENTS.

E. Brown Jr Lith

M^{RS} BARNEY WILLIAMS as
JEMIMA LACARAPEE.

FRENCH'S
AMERICAN DRAMA.
The Acting Edition.

No. LXXVIII.

————◆————

OUR JEMIMY:

OR,

CONNECTICUT COURTSHIP.

A FARCE, IN ONE ACT.

WRITTEN EXPRESSLY FOR MRS. BARNEY WILLIAMS.

BY

H. J. CONWAY.

TO WHICH ARE ADDED,

A Description of the Costume—Cast of the Characters—Entrances and Exits—
Relative Positions of the Performers on the Stage, and the whole of the
Stage Business.

AS PERFORMED AT THE BROADWAY THEATRE, N. Y.

NEW-YORK:

SAMUEL FRENCH,

131 NASSAU-STREET.

Cast of the Characters.—(Our Jemimy.)

AS PERFORMED AT THE

	Broadway, N. Y.	Walnut-st., Phil.
Uncle Joab, (a man of invention,)....Mr. Whiting.		Mr. A'Becket.
Hon. Aug. Gas, (a man of words,).... " Grosvenor.		" Fitzgerald.
Twitcher, } *(an unbeliever of the man of words.)*	" Hodges.	" Wallis.
Deacon Peek, } *Post-master of New Canaan—a man of inquiry,)*.....	" Henry.	" Le Moyne.
Cæsar, (a black man,)............ " Vincent.		" Eberle.
Aunt Jemimy, (one of her sex,).Mrs. Henry.		Mrs. Stoneall.
Our Jemimy. (one of the gals,). " Bar'y Williams.		" B. Williams.
Mrs. Bonnet. (one of the wives,).Miss Duckworth.		Miss Phillipps.

Children, Guests, &c.

SCENE—New Canaan, Connecticut.

COSTUMES OF THE DAY.

OUR JEMIMY.

ACT I.

Scene I.—*A front apartment in* Uncle Joab's *house.—Enter* Caesar, l. h., *counting on his fingers.*

Caesar. Tree—four—five; five, dat's de ole Squire—and dat's all ob de upper class ob de sciety ob New Canaan. Den comes de ole Deacon—dat is de Deacon. What was de Deacon before de Deacon? What am de Deacon? Was made de Deacon and all de odder common white folks makes?

Enter Uncle, r. h.

Uncle. Well, Caesar, will all the folks be here?

Caesar. Will dem? Won't dem?—I guess dem will : dem all knows what dis chile am as de cook, and Miss Jemimy as de—

Uncle. Our Jemima; call her our Jemima. Now my sister, Miss Jemima Primrose, is staying with us, you must call her our Jemima.

Caesar. Berry well; our Jemimy am de Jemimy dat can make de best pies and de best puddin, and de—

Uncle. I know, I know. Now tell me, did you call at the Post Office?

Caesar. I didn't forget dat, because I had to get de brandy from de Deacon's to make de—

Uncle. And you got a letter for me?

Caesar. No. But de Deacon himself hab'em for you, and he say he must gib de letter to you wit his own hands; and here he is coming. And now I is going to de kitchen, [*crossing* r.] Golly Massa, but your churn will hab de grand christinin dis night. It takes dis chile and our Jemimy. [*Exit* r. h.

Enter Deacon Peek, l. h., *with large sealed package.*

Uncle. So it's come, Deacon? it's come, eh?

Deacon. Ay! and sealed like a State packet from Washington.

Uncle. [*Takes packet; reads.*] "To Joab Primrose." [*Opens packet; takes out a silver medal.*] Yes; and here's the medal. Mine's the prize. [*Reads.*] " Prize-Medal awarded to Joab Primrose, for his original double action self-propelling rotary motion churn." Yes, here is the whole description of it in full. And here is the Prize-Medal. I knew it! I knew it! It takes us Connecticut folks to do such things slick; eh, Deacon?

Deacon. Well, yes; particularly in wooden notions.

Uncle. Such as Clocks, Nutmegs, and Hams, eh? Ah! but there is no humbug about my Patent Churn. No, no; it is a real genuine, original invention, and is bound to astonish folks.

Deacon. Well, I did hear it wasn't all your own invention, tho'.

Uncle. Oh! you mean our Jemimy had a hand in it? I won't deny she did give me one thing towards it.

Deacon. And that *one* thing was the idee!

Uncle. Certainly, our Jemimy first gave the idea; but what is an idea if it be not used?—nothing! no! I used the idea.

Deacon. Humph! there is something in that. Talking of idees, I have an idee. I have something here that will surprise you a leetle. Here, [*taking out another sealed letter from his pocket.*] here's another letter with a big seal on it.

Uncle. [*Takes it; reads address.*] " Miss Jemima Primrose!" More luck! This must be for our Jemima. She had two purses and two pairs of knitted stockings at the fair, and—

Deacon. Aye! but the seal ain't the same as yourn.

Uncle. What of that? You don't expect the seal to a regular original invention will be the same as to only a purse or a stocking knitter, do you?

Deacon. Well, there may be something in that.

Uncle. Yes, it must be for our Jemima. [*Calls,* R. H.] Here, Jemima! our Jemima!

Jem. [*From kitchen, as if below.*] Hello! what neow?

Uncle. Come here!

Jem. Can't du it. I'm mixing the dough, and a rollin on it out for the dough-nuts and the punkin pies.

Uncle. [*Bawls.*] Never mind the pies, come!

Jem. Gosh, all conscience! what is't?

Uncle. It is of more consequence than pumpkin pies; come!

Jem. [*Speaks as she enters,* R. H.; *has a long home-spun or check bib apron on, a rolling pin in one hand and a lump of dough in the other, flour on her face, &c.*] Wal, I'm coming. Of more consequence than punkin pies? What in all—[*Sees Deacon; hides rolling pin and dough behind her.*] Gosh! all conscience! there's Peeknose. [*Curtsies to him.*] Heow d'ye do, Deacon? [*Aside, to her father.*] What on arth did you call me out of the kitchen for, and me in this muss?

Uncle. Look at that! [*Shows medal.*

Jem. What is't?

Uncle. The Prize-Medal for my Patent Churn.

Jem. Du tell! It's come, is't? Wal, I'm peaky glad of it.

Uncle. And here's another for you. [*Shows letter.*

Jem. What, for my idee about it?

Uncle. No, no; for your purses and stockings.

Jem. Want tu know. [*Putting rolling pin into one of her apron pockets and the dough in the other; takes the letter.*] What's this on the outside on't? A seal with—

Uncle. Never mind the seal; look inside.

Jem. [*Opens letter; starts; stares.*] Gosh, all conscience! massy me!

Uncle. What is it?

Jem. Wal, if ever!—This ain't about pusses and stockings.

Uncle. No! What then?

Jem. Why, about—[*Stops suddenly; looks at Deacon.*] 'Tain't no matter.

Uncle. But it is some matter. I wish to know what the letter is about.

Deacon. Yes, your father wishes to know what it is all about.

Jem. Fathers ain't the only folks that wish to know suthin about other folks' business. Neow, this is private and my own business, and I always mind my own business and no other folks' business; and as eenamost everybody has some business tu attend tu of their own, I recommend everybody to go about their own business. Don't you think I am right, Deacon?

Deacon. Well, there may be somethirg in that. [*Aside.*] No getting much out of her. Good day, Uncle Joab; good day, Jemima. [*Aside.*] I'll find out what's inside that letter yet. [*Exit,* L. H.

Jem. Peeknose. [*Looks after him.*] Father!—what, do you think? this letter ain't for me.

Uncle. How?

Jem. No!—it's for Aunt Jemimy.

Uncle. Aunt Jemima? What's it about?

Jem. Love!

Uncle. No!

Jem. Yes! [*Looks at letter.*] Wal, if ever! Gosh, all conscience! [*Laughs.*

Uncle. Can't be possible!

Jem. Tell you it is. Hear tu it. [*Reads.*] "Queen of my heart—"

Uncle. Of whose heart?

Jem. Du be patient, du! Hear tu it. [*Reads.*] "The refulgent and matured beauty—" Shouldn't wonder if Aunt Jemimy ever had any beauty, if it ain't come to maturity at sixty-two!

Uncle. Jemima, do read, this is serious.

Jem. Considerable serious, I should think.

Uncle. Now, Jemima—

Jem. [*Reads.*] "Matured beauty of thy charms has made a deep and lasting impression on my heart, and lighted a fire therein which, if not speedily allayed by thy dear self, will burst forth and consume my mortal part, leaving naught but a heap of ashes as a momenti mori of him who died for thee, and who, while living, was thy devoted slave. Augustus Gas."

Uncle. Gas, Gas! Who's he?

Jem. Why, the spirit of his burning ashes, I guess. But here's a P. S. [*Reads.*] "P. S. With your kind permission, I shall kiss your hand at New Canaan on Monday next. I shall expect an answer at the P. O."

Uncle. What is the meaning of it?

Jem. Meaning on't? Guess it don't take much head work to cypher it out: it speaks plainly for itself. Aunt Jemimy has picked up a beau in York; and he's coming down here tu spark her. Don't you hear he's in a flame already?

Uncle. What! sister Jemima going to make such a fool of herself! Can't be possible!

Jem. Heow so?

Uncle. What! a beau at sixty-two? It's downright madness. Besides, she has 25,000 dollars Rail Road Stock.

Jem. That's it! That makes Aunt Jemimy's beauty refulgent and consuming.

Uncle. But the money must not go out of the family. I have for years looked upon it as good as ours. Oh, it's all confounded nonsense! This fellow Gas must be a swindler. It can never be! It shall never be!

Jem. Wal, father, you are great at inventions: invent something to make an old woman confess she is old, and unfit to receive the addresses, or to marry a young man. Take out a patent for it, and your fortune's made. This accounts for the extra chickens and pies for her supper to-night.

Uncle. What do you mean?

Jem. Why, aunt Jemimy sent for me tu her room tu-day, and asked what all the preparation for supper was about, and I told her it was on account of christening your Patent Churn, and that a hull heap of gals and fellers was expected. [*Imitates.*] "Gals and fellers!" ses she; "Jemimy, why don't you learn to express yourself with propriety? Don't call visitors at this house gals and fellers." "Wal," ses I, "I won't. What be they tu be called?" "Ladies and gentlemen," ses she. Ses I, "du tell: but I'll remember. But any how, gals and fellers comes more natral-like." "Wal, then," ses she, "Jemimy, I wish you would have an extry pair of chickens nicely briled, and a couple of pies or so for me. I shall sup in my own apartment, and you can let Nelly wait on us." "Us?" ses I. "Yes, me and my guest," ses she. "Guest?" ses I: "du I know her?" Then she kind o' snickered and looked down, and fidgetted like a hen on hot cinders; and jist then Nell yauped out from the kitchen-stairs that the pot of lasses candy was bilin' over, and I run down. So I didn't hear who she expected, but to-day is Monday, and no doubt it is this Gas.

Uncle. What is to be done? If she should take it into her fool's head to marry, we shall lose her money, and I have calculated on it to help me in my inventions.

Jem. Neow's the time for your invention tu operate. Invent something tu keep this young Gas from flaring up with aunt Jemimy's money.

Uncle. Aye, that's it! No doubt the fellow's an adventurer—a swindler—a scoundrel—if one could only find it out. What's to be done, Jemimy?

Jem. Wal, I don't know. Guess it don't take a power of invention tu understand human nature; and if you should find out Gas is a swindler, 'twould be hard to convince aunt Jemimy of it, as long as Gas makes believe he is consuming with love for her.

Uncle. That's true.

Jem. If he's only poor and wants aunt's money, guess that don't constitoote swindlin'?

Uncle. That's true again. What is to be done?—I havn't an idea.

Jem. Can't you invent one?

Uncle. No; not at a moment's warning: if I only had time ——

Jem. Wal, maybe by the time this Gas has hitched teams with aunt Jemimy, you'll invent suthin' tu unhitch 'em—eh? Wal, if you can't, I can.

Uncle. How?—what?

Jem. Wal, this is it: You remember last New-Year's, when I dressed up like aunt Jemimy and made calls, and fooled all the folks round, and you among 'em, you never found out 'twas me till I told you?

Uncle. I remember.

Jem. Didn't I act out aunty complete?

Uncle. You did.

Jem. And everybody said it took our Jemimy tu do it. And I can du it again. I'll dress up like aunty again, receive this Gas in her place, and if I don't give him enough of aunt Jemimy and make him as sick of her as a bed-bug of Lyons' Magnetic Powder, say our Jemimy don't know beans.

Uncle. But what's to become of sister Jemimy?

Jem. Oh, I have invented suthin' for her too. Guess she'll start for York pretty quick.

Uncle. For York? How?

Jem. You'll see. All you have tu do is to work out my idees. [*Looks at letter*]. The P. S. says he expects an answer at the P. O. Neow I'll write one as if from aunt Jemima; you give it to the Deacon, and tell him to deliver it with his own hands, as it's of consequence. That's enough for the Deacon: guess we shall soon hear something about this Gas.

Uncle. That's a good idea—the Deacon, once on the scent, won't leave it till he finds out.

Jem. Where he was raised, what's his business, heow much he's worth, where he stays, and what he expects to have for dinner. Wal, neow, you come for the letter, then I'll to aunty and give her the first dose of Gas. [*Exit,* R. H.

Uncle. What a girl our Jemimy is for ideas, and what an old fool my sister Jemima is to think of marrying at her time of life and throwing away her money on a young fellow who would no doubt squander it in all sorts of folly and dissipation. [*Exit,* R. H. E.

SCENE II.—AUNT JEMIMY'S *room,* D. F. R. H.—*Screen,* L. O.—*Toilet-table,* R. H., *with glass, &c., and very large pair of scissors.—Chairs.*—AUNT JEMIMY *discovered attudinizing before the glass.—She has red ringlets, red nose, &c.—A cap trimmed with flowers and ribbons.—Extravagantly dressed.—Attempting juvenility.*

Aunty. I do resemble the fashions for June. This auburn hair is very becoming, it matches the trimming of my cap, and tends to soften the natural glow of my complexion; and the cap is, as the milliner said, a perfect love of a cap. I really do think that milliner a woman of great taste. She assured me, and my glass confirms her assurance, that in it I don't look over twenty or twenty-five at the most. How shall I receive him—languishingly seated—or rising gracefully, swim towards him as he enters? [*Practices*]. I do feel a little nervous at meeting my Augustus for the first time in daylight. That screen, however, softens the glare of light from the window. I think I will receive him sitting. [*Sits*]. One foot—I have often been complimented on my feet—protruding a little, thus— but, bless me! I had forgotten; he promised to write. I must send to the post-office—I must send there. [*Rises—calls,* R. H.] Jemima! Jemima! I wish to gracious brother Joab hadn't named his girl after me; but I have always insisted upon a proper distinction being made between us. I am always addressed as Miss Jemima, and she as Our Jemima. Jemima! [*Calling, and exit* R. H.*

Enter JEMIMY, R. H., *without her apron.*

Jem. Did you yaup out for me, aunty?

Aunty. Yaup out for you, child! Don't use such expressions, and don't call me aunty, but Miss Jemimy.

Jem. Wal, I won't, aunty—that is, Miss Jemimy. [*Looks at her admiringly.*] Gosh! all gracious! Powers o' massy!

Aunty. What is it, child?

Jem. Be this you, aunty—Miss Jemimy, I mean? [*Walks around her.*

Aunty. You admire my dress, eh?

Jem. Dress! Wal, guess I du admire it.

Aunty. It is becoming this cap, eh?

Jem. That cap caps all I ever did see!

Aunty. You think my taste improved since my visit to York?

Jem. Wonderful! Why, heow you du look! Gosh! all gracious! ain't you slick!

Aunty. Now, Jemimy, I am going to ask you a question.

Jem. Yes, aunty—Miss Jemima.

Aunty. Now observe me. [*Walks.*] How old do you really think I look?

Jem. [*Making believe she understands her literally.*] Oh! I know exactly tu the hour how old you be—it's sot down ——

Aunty. Pooh! pooh!

Jem. In our bible ——

* The rest of this scene is sometimes omitted.

Aunty. Never mind ——

Jem. Jemimy Primrose, born 8th June, 17 hundred ——

Aunty. Nonsense, child! Seventeen hundred, indeed! That was your grand aunt, Jemimy—not me.

Jem. Oh! ah! du tell! Of course it must be, neow I look at you, Miss Jemimy: you can't be more than sixteen, or sixteen and a half.

Aunty. Oh, yes, yes—more, more.

Jem. Wal, then, seventeen. I can't allow you more than that without making your mother a baby.

Aunty. She was very young.

Jem. It runs in the family—all the Jemimy's are always young.

Aunty. Always look so—yes; but I don't want to conceal my age. I own to 28.

Jem. [*Aside.*] Not half. Why, aunty—Miss Jemimy—you don't say!

Aunty. Yes, child, 28; though I have always passed for less.

Jem. No doubt, for many years! I hev always sed, and du wonder, why aunty—that is, Miss Jemimy—don't get married.

Aunty. I have always considered early marriages improper.

Jem. I hev time and agin sed to myself, Wal, if I was a feller ——

Aunty. Feller!

Jem. That is, a young chap ——

Aunty. Chap!

Jem. I mean, man—I would shin up tu aunty ——

Aunty. Shin up!

Jem. Wal, then—spark her.

Aunty. And do you suppose that I, with my delicacy and refinement, and who have had the advantage of visiting large cities— Boston and New York—could admit the addresses of county louts!

Jem. No—sartin; but then some of them city fellers—chaps—I mean, young men, might —

Aunty. And how do you know they have not! My charms are not destined to bloom and fade unnoticed. No; I am now the admiration of one of the handsomest of his sex—yes.

Jem. [*Aside.*] Now it's coming! Du tell.

Aunty. Yes—young and handsome.

Jem. Want tu know!—a Yorker!

Aunty. No—he is an Englishman—a baronet—and heir to a lord.

Jem. Gosh! all gracious! Heir to a lord!—what lord!

Aunty. The lord Nozoo!—of a very ancient family.

Jem. Wal, only to think on't!—heir to the lord Nozoo, and no doubt has a powerful sight of money.

Aunty. Will have, when he takes possession of his estates: at present he's a minor.

Jem. A miner! Oh, he digs gold in Californy, eh!

Aunty. Jemimy, you seem to be more stupid than ever. No, no; he is not of age: as soon as he is, he will take possession of his castles and estates.

Jem. Castles and estates! Where be they!

Aunty. In Ayrshire and the Isle of Sky.

Jem. I shouldn't wonder! And when-is't to be?

Aunty. When he's of age.

Jem. Oh, then you ain't to have him till then?

Aunty. [*Sighs and smiles.*] I don't know. I have seen him but three times, but he is so importunate that I fear I can't hold out.

Jem. Seen him only three times! He must be a snoudger to spark.

Aunty. A what?

Jem. A snoudger.

Aunty. Jemimy!

Jem. I mean a team——

Aunty. A team!

Jem. Wal, he must'r hitched close at once.

Aunty. Jemimy, I beg you will use different expressions when alluding to the interviews between that gentleman and myself. I have seen him but three times—once in an omnibus, once at the museum, and once at the hotel, and there——

Jem. Wal.

Aunty. He made me promise to receive his visits here.

Jem. [*Aside.*] Guess I know enough now. [*Aloud.—Sighs deeply.*] Heigho! Wal, I du think it is too bad! [*Whimpers.*]

Aunty. What is too bad?

Jem. Why, that things should act so contrary with me. [*Begins to cry.*] Everybody has beaus and keeps 'em but me. There was Hezekiah Huckleberry—he sparked me for more than six months; then he quit and went to Californy; but that warn't nothing. Here neow I hev made sich preparation for supper, and when the time comes everybody will be happy but me. Them consarned railroads—I du wish from my heart there warn't none of 'em.

Aunty. What are you talking about?

Jem. Why, the accident.

Aunty. What accident?

Jem. The railroad accident. Why, ain't you hern? Oh, my poor Ebenezer! [*Cries.*]

Aunty. Well, never mind; I havn't time to listen. I wish you to go to the post-office.

Jem. 'Taint no use. The mail ain't arrived—all smashed up—poor Ebenezer!

Aunty. The mail smashed!

Jem. And the passengers! Oh, my poor Ebenezer! [*Bursts out.*]

Aunty. Mail and passengers smashed! When—where?

Jem. Why, this day—the train from York—all smashed; but nobody ain't to blame. Oh, my Ebenezer!

Aunty. From York?

Jem. Yes, the train with the freight got stuck someheow—nobody knows heow—and the next passenger train come full chissel kerchunk agin it. Oh, my poor Ebenezer!

Aunty. Were many hurt?

Jem. Heaps! but they du say one young feller was a sight tu see, and pitiful to hear him cry out, "Oh, my legs! Oh, my Jemimy!"

Aunty. A young man coming from York?

Jem. Yes; but they couldn't get nothing out of him up tu his faintin' away but "Oh, my legs! Oh, my Jemima!" But after he was insensible, and the doctor sed his two legs must both come off, they looked on his velise, and there they see his name. Oh, my poor Ebenezer!

Aunty. Poor Ebenezer, indeed! I was apprehensive it might have been my poor Augustus.

Jem. [*Very suddenly.*] What! Did you say Augustus?

Aunty. I did.

Jem. Don't—don't!

Aunty. Don't what? You alarm me!

Jem. Don't say the young feller's name that loves you is Augustus.

Aunty. Why not?

Jem. Because his other name might be the same as was on his velise.

Aunty. And that was——

Jem. Gas! [AUNTY *shrieks—falls into chair—kicks.*] She's off! Gas exploded her! Aunt Jemimy! [*Runs to table and brings bottle.*] Snift o' this—she can't! [*Slaps her hands, &c.—Runs and fetches water and throws it in her face.*]

Aunty. Oh! [*Sighs and recovers.*] Oh, his legs!—his dear legs!

Jem. Don't take on so! maybe they ain't both broke off, or if they be, a handsome young feller with cork legs ain't tu be sneezed at.

Aunty. Oh, my Augustus! Oh, his dear legs! What shall I do! What shall I do?

Jem. Wal, if it was me I should go and see for myself what's left of him may be worth preserving. But my poor Ebenezer, he's smashed all tu bits.

Aunty. You are right, Jemima—I will go.

Jem. But the cars won't start till——

Aunty. The cars!—don't name the horrid things to me! I'll never travel by them again. Oh! my poor dear Augustus!—the charming infant, to lose his precious legs! But I'll go.

Jem. Du—go to him—but I wouldn't go in that dress. I'd put on a kind of half mourning for the sake of his lost legs.

Aunty. True—his dear legs! Come and assist me. [*Crosses to* R.] Oh, my poor Augustus! [*Exit,* R. H.

Jem. [*As she follows out.*] Oh, Gas!

SCENE III.—*An apartment in a Hotel at New Canaan.*

Enter the Honorable AUGUSTUS *fashionably dressed, and* TWITCHER *in livery,* L. H.

Aug. What a confounded inquisitive fellow that landlord is. He eyed me so closely I began to fear he smoked us.

Twitcher. Us?—why he never saw me before.

Aug. And it's over three years since he saw me, and who the devil could have dreamt of finding him here?

Twitcher. Pugh! if he never knew you but as Bob Bonnet, I defy him to recognize you now as the Honorable Augustus Gas.

Aug. I don't know. Circumstances stamp recollections, unfortunately. But when I left him, I left something behind me that might turn up against me.

Twitcher. What was that?

Aug. A wife!

Twitcher. The devil!

Aug. Exactly, most of them are.

Twitcher. There is no fear of Mrs B.

Aug. However, no time must be lost; I must visit this ancient spinster without delay, whisk her off to New York, get some magistrate to tack us together.

Twitcher. The ceremony won't be very binding.

Aug. Touch her railroad stock.

Twitcher. In which I go halves.

Aug. Why, that is our agreement; but in this case I ought to have two-thirds, as I shall have the old woman on my hands.

Twitcher. For how long? No, no, a bargain is a bargain. I am to have one-half, or I declare off, and will blow you to Mrs. B. If it had been my month to play master and you man, why then I should have stood in your shoes, nay, running a greater risk.

Aug. Greater risk! How so?

Twitcher. Why I have two wives already.

Aug. Well, I might put my four children against one of your wives; but no matter. Time is precious; now go to the post-office for the divine Jemima's answer to my letter.

Deacon. [*Outside*, L. H.] In No. 8. Very well. [*Knocks outside.*

Aug. Who the devil is this? Now for the honorable again. Ah! Twitcher, see who's at the door. [TWITCHER *goes to door.*

Enter DEACON, L. H.

Deacon. [*Bows.*] Do I speak to the Honorable Augustus Gas, Esquire?

Aug. That is me! plain honorable, without the superfluous esquire.

Deacon. Member of Congress, I reckon?

Aug. I am sorry to say, you reckon without your host.

Deacon. One of the members of the Patent Office, at Washington, no doubt.

Aug. I have not that honor; not connected with any patent but the patent of nobility. May I presume to guess your business with me Mr. a-a—what's your name?

Deacon. Deacon Peek, Postmaster of New Canaan. I always make it a point of delivering letters of consequence, or letters to persons of consequence, personally. By chance, being in the office below, I saw your honorable name in the book, and having just received this letter for your honorable self, I took the liberty of bringing it myself.

[*Hands letter to* TWITCHER, *who dusts it, and hands it to* AUGUSTUS.

Aug. [*Opening letter.*] Charming creature! dear divinity! I fly to wait upon you, [*crosses to* L. H.] Twitcher!

Twitcher. Sir!

Aug. Pay the individual for the letter. Remain here, till I return. Au revoir, individual. Twitcher, remember. [*Exits, L. H., singing.*

Twitcher. [*Aside.*] Remember! yes, I shall, that you are too great a rascal to lose sight of; so I shall take the liberty of following you. [*Crosses to L. H. to DEACON.*] Au revoir individual—they will pay you at the bar. Remember. [*Exits, L. H.*

Deacon. [*Imitates.*] Pay me at the bar. Very mysterious. Not from Washington—not from the Patent Office. I'll inquire of the landlord—he is not very communicative—but I'll tell him it is none of my business, merely to oblige a friend; yes, there's something in that. [*Exit, R. H.*

SCENE IV.—AUNTY'S *Apartment as before.*

Enter UNCLE *and* CAESAR, R. H.

Uncle. And show the gentleman to this room directly he comes.
Caesar. Yes, sar.
Uncle. You remember his name!
Caesar. Yes, sar. De Honorable Disgusting Gash, Esquire.
Uncle. And if any of the other folks come, you show them into the parlor.
Caesar. Yes, sar; but how can de supper be sarved if Miss Jemimy aint dar; you see dat gal, Nelly, aint nothing, and dis chile cant do ebberyting.
Uncle. I tell you, long before supper-time, Miss Jemima will be there.
Caesar. You see, massa, dars de ole lady, de odder Miss Jemimy, she am to hab her supper here; Nelly must wait upon her, because de ole woman she cant bear dis nigger, and golly, dar aint much lub lost, for dis chile does hate de ole ——
Uncle. Hush! she is here.

Enter, R. H., JEMIMA, *dressed exactly like her Aunt.*

Jem. [*Fan, &c.*] Brother! how often have I said I would not have that nigger in my room—the odor is offensive. Pah! Leave the room, black man.
Caesar. [*Half aside.*] If I is, you is white trash. If she come down star, I be dam if I don't pin de dish-cloth on her tail. [*Exit, L. H.*
Jem. [*Laughs.*] There, you see, Caesar thinks I am the real genuine article. Heou du I look! [*Walks, imitating.*
Uncle. Jemima, you do beat all. If I didn't know you to be our Jemima, I would swear you was sister.
Jem. Well, now, you remember your part of this play, when the time comes, and you hear me yaup out, you rush in, and do as I told you.
Uncle. All right; and when sister Jemima returns, I will keep her from seeing any one till you are ready for her to appear, and——
Caesar. [*Outside.*] Dis way, sar; the missusses' room am dis way.
Jem. [*Sits in attitude.*] Here comes the honorable: now, father, clear. [*Exit UNCLE, R. H.*

14*

Enter CAESAR, L. H., *showing in* AUGUSTUS.

Caesar. De Honorable Disgusting Gash to see de ole woman.

Aug. Old woman, you scoundrel—[CAESAR *runs out.*] what does the fellow mean? [*advances.*] Can I realize my happiness? Does my charming Jemima permit her devoted Augustus to kiss her fair hand, [*takes it—kisses it—she eyes him over her fan.*] and openly avow his passion?

Jem. [*simpering.*] Oh! I fear I am very indiscreet to admit you to such familiarity after so brief an acquaintance.

Aug. Brief an acquaintance. Love takes no account of time; once it takes root it springs up to maturity; with me, it is consuming passion. Oh, let me not perish with the flame!

Jem. How am I to prevent it?

Aug. By promising to bless me with full possession of those charms.

Jem. And would you really make me believe the little beauty I possess.

Aug. Little beauty! Oh! do not wrong your charms—full, ripe, glowing charms.

Jem. Oh!

Aug. Which to gaze on would warm an anchorite.

Jem. Oh!

Aug. Nay, would infuse life into a petrefaction.

Jem. Flatterer!

Aug. Flattery—no! Truth! My lips utter naught but the dictates of my heart; it flows as naturally as beauty beams from those eyes.

Jem. [*Aside*] Guess he's some pumpkins at sparking, anyhow. [*Aloud, languishingly.*] Ah! I hardly know how to trust you—you men-creatures are so deceitful to us poor maidens. I fear there's no believing you. Would you—would you deceive a poor weak, silly maid like me?

Aug. On my knees I swear.   [*Going to kneel.*

Jem. No, don't swear—don't kneel. I—I—believe you [*Aside.*] are lying.

Aug. And you will bless me with that fair hand.

Jem. If I should consent, you will carry me to Europe?

Aug. By the first steamer.

Jem. And introduce me to your noble family? ·

Aug. Instantly.

Jem. But your father—the Lord—Lord ——

Aug. Nozoo. He would receive you with raptures.

Jem. And if you succeed to the title, shall I be my Lady Nozoo?

Aug. As surely as I shall be the Lord Nozoo. [*Aside.*] That's true.

Jem. And your sisters?—you said you had sisters.

Aug. [*Aside.*] Did I?—damme, I forget. Yes, my sisters ——

Jem. Arabella Wilhelmina and Julianna Malvina you told me were their names.

Aug. [*Aside*] Curse me if I recollect. Yes, both sweet, kind, good-tempered girls.

Jem. And about my own age?

Aug. Just about.

Jem. Sweet young things! I am sure I shall love them for my Augustus's sake. Oh, Augustus! if you are deceiving me, you will break my heart. Think how I have, at such a very, very short notice, bestowed upon you my first, my maiden affections—on you, an unknown foreigner! Oh! I fear, I fear I have been too rash. Augustus! don't, don't take advantage of my youthful innocence—don't, don't! [*Sobs on his shoulder.*]

Aug. [*Aside.*] Youthful innocence! My darling girl ——

Jem. [*Sobs.*] Oh! oh! oh!

Aug. Calm yourself!

Jem. [*Recovers a little.*] But to leave my home—my country—for a stranger's country—a stranger's home—to leave my brother—my—my—my—but you will be all to me—won't you, Augustus?

Aug. Yes.

Jem. My country?

Aug. Yes.

Jem. My home?

Aug. Yes.

Jem. My brother—my husband—my all? Oh! [*Falls into his arms, sobbing.*]

Aug. [*Aside.*] This is too affecting. My Jemimy!

Jem. I can't help it; I am a creature of feeling. Forgive your Jemimy. But to be thus loved, at such a very short notice—and for myself alone ——

Aug. [*Aside.*] And your Railroad Stock! Can my Jemimy ask?—does she doubt her Augustus?

Jem. Nay—you are handsome, with youth, beauty and wealth, and to love a maid like me, possessing nothing but my poor personal charms. [*Aside.*] Guess my gab is equal to his.

Aug. Nay—nay, you shall not undervalue your own fortune, for though it is but small ——

Jem. [*Aside.*] Neow the touchstone! A poor five hundred dollars.

Aug. Five hundred dollars!

Jem. In the Bank of New Canaan.

Aug. Ah! now you would deceive me—though the amount shall all be settled on yourself—still you know it is twenty-five thousand dollars.

Jem. [*Aside.*] I'm tickling him. [*Aloud.*] Twenty-five thousand dollars! Oh, generous man, and have you taken this delicate method of enriching the poor Jemimy Primrose? Oh, you dear man!

Aug. Call it not generosity, only justice—'tis but just your own property should be settled upon you.

Jem. And which is five hundred dollars!

Aug. [*Half alarmed.*] Twenty-five thousand dollars, New York and Erie Railroad Stock, in the name of Jemimy Primrose of New Canaan, Conn. I read it in the books myself.

Jem. [*Aside.*] I guessed so. [*Aloud.*] Yes; but that Jemima is not me.

Aug. Not you!

Jem. No, dearest—that's Our Jemimy.

Aug. Our Jemimy!—who's she?

Jem. My niece—a little chit of a child—a perfect baby—whose charms are not refulgent and matured like those of your own Jemima.

Aug. [*Aside.*] The devil! This is the wrong Jemimy; I must declare off.

Jem. Augustus, dear—you are silent—speak!

Aug. [*Aside.*] What the devil shall I say?—the money is in the family.

Jem. You know my tenderness of heart! Oh, speak, speak!—say you love me still! Speak, Augustus—speak!

Aug. Madam!

Jem. [*Breaking out.*] I call him Augustus! and he calls me Madam! Oh! oh! [*Screams.*] Ah! he loves me no longer! I cannot endure the shock—my heart is bursting! Oh! oh! [*Going to fall into his arms—he turns from her—she nearly falls—recovers herself.*] Wretch! —perjured villain!—you have broken my heart! Yes, it is broken —I feel it all in little bits. I am dying; but I will not die alone! [*Seizes him—drags him to toilet-table—takes up very large pair of scissors.*]

Aug. Take care! What the devil are you about?

Jem. About to sacrifice you, monster of deception, to the just revenge of a deceived yet doating maiden!

Aug. Help! murder! [*Breaks from her—she chases him—*Caesar *enters—she knocks him down.—Rushes at* Augustus.—Uncle *enters,* r. h., *stays her hand.—She falls into chair.—Kicks.—Screams.*]

SCENE CLOSES.

Scene V.—*A chamber in* Uncle Joab's *house.—Door in flat opens,* l. h., *and* Twitcher *peeps in, then enters.*

Twitcher. I have got into the house unseen by anybody but the nigger, and I am determined I won't leave it without the Honorable Gas. Ah! here he comes. I'll hide and watch him. If seen, I must brazen it out. [*Goes into door flat,* r.; *listens.*

Enter Augustus, r. h.

Aug. A precious spec I had nearly made of Miss Jemima. Confound it! How the deuce could I know there were two Jemima Primroses, and that the young one owns the Stock? Couldn't I make love to the young one? As the old lady has left the house, and the old gentleman seems easily gulled, I'll get an introduction to our Jemima. Let me see how shall I manage it. [Uncle Joab *speaks without.*] Oh! here he comes. Now, invention, assist me!

Enter Uncle, r. h.

Uncle. [*Aside.*] Now, to work out Jemima's second idea. [*Aloud.*] Well, sir, what am I to think of this insult to my sister?

Aug. Insult! Insult, my dear sir! You mean mistake! merely a mistake on her part. Has not the lady told you—

Uncle. Told me! Yes; she said she would not stay another moment under the same roof with such a villain, such a deceiver; and has left my house.

Aug. Permit me to explain.

Uncle. If you please.

Aug. [*Aside.*] Now for an extemporaneous hit. [*Aloud.*] Being at the fair of the American Institute of New York with some friends of mine, amongst other inventions—all of which do honor to the enterprising citizens of this great country—I saw a Patent Churn which struck me, I being in the agricultural interest.

Twitcher. [*Aside.*] Used a shovel two years in a State prison.

Aug. Which churn struck me as far superior to any churn I had ever seen or heard of. The name of the inventor was Joab Primrose, of New Canaan.

Uncle. I am that—

Aug. [*Interrupting blandly.*] Permit me. I had hardly read the name aloud, when one of my friends cried: "By Gad! Augustus, my boy! that is the very family you ought to get acquainted with. I am personally acquainted with that family, sir, and I—"

Uncle. Ah! indeed! And his name is?

Aug. Yes, exactly. His name is—let me see—it wasn't Switchell!

Uncle. Switchell! No; I don't know Switchell.

Aug. No; of course, you don't. Switchell is an Englishman—came over with me. Devilish good fellow, but prejudiced, confoundedly prejudiced against this country. No; it wasn't Switchell! no; it was—what a shocking memory I have; but, indeed, I had only been introduced to my friend—

Uncle. Whose name you forget.

Aug. My friend said so much in favor of the Primroses, that I begged a letter of introduction. We adjourned to my hotel. And there, whilst my friend wrote the letter, I looked over the book of arrivals; and, lo! what should I see, but the name of Miss Jemima Primrose! [*Very loud.*] To make a long story short, I instantly determined to obtain an introduction to the lady; sent up my card—there's one. [*Hands one to* UNCLE.] Pretty, ain't they? Family crest, ariel castle, Truth in a well. I was admitted. In a short conversation, discovered the old lady had a niece.

Uncle. Oh! oh!

Aug. Came down here for the purpose of engaging the aunt's good offices—old lady misunderstood—imagined I was making love to herself—a mistake, of course. You know, my dear sir, it was impossible I could make love to her—fine old lady, no doubt—but old enough to be my mother—all a mistake!

Uncle. [*Aside.*] What a confounded crammer! but our Jemima will be even with him. [*Aloud.*] Well, sir, as you seem very desirous of being united to my family, spoken of so highly by your friend, whose name you don't recollect, I shall be happy to introduce you to our Jemima.

Aug. Our Jemima?

Uncle. My daughter; but who is entirely her own mistress, and has all her property at her own disposal.

Twitcher. Oh! oh!

Aug. Property, my dear sir, don't mention it. So, you give me our Jemima, and I am satisfied.

Uncle. All you have to do is to gain her own consent. We have a little party of country folks this evening, I shall be happy to introduce you, if you will condescend to honor them with your company.

Aug. My dear Primrose!—excuse my familiarity, but when I take a liking, I hate ceremony—my dear Primrose, country society I am anxious to cultivate. I hope our Jemima is not city bred.

Uncle. Never saw a city, never left her home. She is a true Connecticut girl; but she will speak for herself: here she comes.

JEMIMA *sings outside and as she enters.—She is now dressed to receive her party.*

> Neow, at last, the day is come,
>   Tooral laddy, &c.
> When the Primroses are some :
>   Tooral laddy, &c.
> Father's churn has got the prize.
>
> > [*Stops suddenly; looks at* GAS.

Uncle. Jemimy, this is the Honorable Augustus Gas, an English gentleman.

Aug. Beg pardon—nobleman. [*Aside.*] What a guy.

Jem. [*Crosses to him; examining him.*] Heow d'ye do, Honorable Gas, nobleman, and no gentleman? You be he, I guess, that come down tu spark Aunt Jemimy?

Aug. All a mistake! entirely a mistake on the part of the old lady, and which I have had the pleasure of explaining to your father's satisfaction.

Jem. Du tell! want tu know? Did the old lady mistake you for a gentleman, when you wasn't none? or heow was it?

Aug. She mistook my intentions.

Jem. No doubt on't.

Aug. Which were merely intercessions for her good offices on my behalf with another lady.

Jem. Want tu know! Another lady? 'Who can she be?

Aug. Yourself!

Jem. Me!

Aug. You!

Jem. Gosh, all conscience! Get out : you ain't in arnest!

Aug. Perfectly so.

Jem. What! you come deown here to New Canaan tu spark me! Why, you never see or heard of me before.

Uncle. Oh! yes, he has : his friend, whose name he forgets, told him all about our family.

Jem. Oh! that, indeed! And so you really hev come deown tu spark me!

Aug. If permitted, to throw myself at your feet.

Jem. Heow!

Aug. There to pour out—

Jem. Hold on! hold on! That ain't our Connecticut fashion of sparking. We don't allow no throwing anybody at our feet, or pouring out nothin' neither. And besides, we never sparks afore folks. If you be in arnest, and are going tu begin, father must clear out.

Aug. [*Aside.*] So much the better. I am in earnest.

Twitcher. [*Aside.*] Not much trouble to fool her.

Jem. Father, clear yourself, and tell the folks I'm a coming just as soon as my new beau has got through his first beginning tu make love tu me. [*Aside to him.*] See the Deacon, he has news, and watch for the old lady. [*Aloud.*] Tell 'em I'm a coming, and will bring my beau along, but for massy sake don't let on he's a nobleman and no gentleman. I must tell 'em that—so clear! [*Exit* UNCLE, R. H. There—neow we're alone.

Aug. [*Aside.*] Now for a flight. My dearest——

Jem. Hold on! I must take a cheer and squat first.

Aug. Squat!

Jem. [*Gets a chair.*—TWITCHER *hides, but she sees him.*] Sartin! Gosh! all conscience! you can't spark Connecticut fashion without you squat down. [*Sits—takes a stocking and needles from her pocket.*] Neow, you must go outside and knock at the door, and when I say Come in! you must come and squat deown too. Neow, clear out!

Aug. [*Aside.*] So this is courting Connecticut fashion! What an idiot she is! [*Exit*, L.

Jem. [*Aside.*] 'Tother chap's listning—guess listners never hear much good of themselves. [*Knock.*] Come in! [*She looks—then pretends to knit.*—*He takes a chair and sits.*] Neow you must say, Heow d'ye do, Jemimy!

Aug. How do you do, Jemimy!

Jem. Then I kinder look at you—so, [*looks half aside*] and snicker [*snicker*], and say, Middling well; heow are you! when you kind o' look at me and say, Dreadful smart, thank'ee.

Aug. [*Imitates.*] Dreadful smart, thank'ee.

Jem. Heow's the weather out! Neow you must hitch up your cheer a leetle mite closer tu me, and say—Wal, it's kind o' fair—or, kind o' not fair, tu dry for the grass—or, tu wet for the hay—or, a kind o' drizzling—or, middlin', as it may be. Neow hitch.

[AUGUSTUS *hitches his chair a little closer.*—*She smirks, &c.*— JEMIMY *hitches her chair, and looks sideways at him.* Then you kinder look, and say, as if yeow meant suthin', Jemimy!

Aug. [*Attempts imitation.*] Jemima!

Jem. Then I give a look as means something, and I say, Ebenezer —I mean, Augustus!—You see Ebenezer comes more natral, as he always sparked me till you come. Wal, then, you say, Won't you have a bite! and then you offer me a hunk of gingerbread.

Aug. But I havn't any.

Jem. Wal, you should oughter hev; but 'tain't no matter: here. [*Gives him two immense apples from her pocket.*] Neow you can hand me one, kinder snickering, and I take it; and neow we both chaw a spell. [*They eat, she casting looks at him, &c.*] Neow I hitch agin, [*hitches*], and say, Hev you hearn the news?

Aug. No!

Jem. That's it. Wal, [*wiping her mouth*] I'll tell it to you. Neow you hitch closer. [*He does.*] There's a French Count, or an English Count, or a Spanish Count, or some other Count of not much account, has come deown tu our town to spark old aunty Debby Higgins, and she over sixty. Neow you must say No, and snicker.

Aug. No! [*Snickers*].

Jem. Yee's! [*laughs*] and I hearn tell the old woman was rotten fool enuff tu 'bleive him.

Aug. No!

Jem. Yee's! [*Laughs.*] Why don't you laugh? You must laugh when I snicker, and guffaw right out when I laugh.

Aug. Yes.

Jem. Yes;—wal, neow, you can give the last hitch to your cheer, and I du tu. [*Hitch.*] Then you look at me kinder anxious like for what's coming next, and I look at you, so [*looks hard at him*], as much as tu say, heow easily old women are fooled. You understand?

Aug. [*Aside.*] Does she smoke? Yes, I understand.

Jem. Wal, then, though old aunty Higgins would hev gin her two ears tu be married tu any he crittur, she was fool enough to spile her own chance.

Aug. [*Naturally anxious.*] How?

Jem. That's jist heow you should talk. Heow? Why, what du you think?—the old crittur was fool enough tu 'bleive what the feller told her—that he really did love her for herself alone, and she over sixty!

Aug. [*Uneasy.*] No!

Jem. Yee's! [*Prolonged.*] He! he! he! Why don't you laugh?

Aug. [*Attempting.*] I do.

Jem. [*Aside.*] On the wrong side of your mouth, I guess. [*Aloud.*] Yee's; and she up and told him she warn't worth a red cent, and he 'blieved she was worth I don't know heow many thousand dollars. Yee's. Then the Count he cleared, and aunty Higgins she went stret off into a conniption fit. Yee's.

Aug. [*Aside.*] All right—she don't smoke!

Jem. Yes, Deacon Peek—you know Deacon Peek?

Aug. Yes, I have seen him.

Jem. He b'longs to the march of intellect busybody association in our town: he knows everybody and everything. He's one of the inquirin' intellectual spirits of this enlightened age. He sees the times neow ain't as they used to was, when the world was contented tu rest in the depths of ignorance. In them times the Deacon ses a feller might kiss a gal and nobody wouldn't talk about it.

Aug. No!

Jem. Yes; and our folks might hev had two pies at one supper, and our nearest neighbor never would hev thought of trying tu find out whether they was mince, custard, plain squash, or pandowdy.

Aug. No!

Jem. Yes; but the Deacon ses t'ain't so neow. Mankind are emerging neow from their benighted ignorance and making stupendous efforts after universal knowledge. It's calculated, in the course of time, the Common Council will find out there's mud in the streets.

Aug. No!

Jem. Yes; and maybe hev it cleared out, but that's uncertain. Yes; and the Deacon ses—Formerly, everybody's business was nobody's business, and oyster-house critics couldn't arn their salt; but neow everybody's business is the business of everybody else. Yes; and the Deacon ses the business of strangers is particularly his business tu find out. Yes; and he allows aunty Higgins got the best on it arter all. Yes; he ses this Count turned out tu be no account, but a swindlin' scoundrel. He ses there's many sich that dress up with whiskers and mustachers as natral as yours be, and make b'lieve tu be Counts and Lords, and so cheat folks out of their money.

Aug. You astonish me!

Jem. I shouldn't wonder. Yes; and the Deacon ses he knows this Count or Lord has got a wife and children already.

Aug. No!

Jem. Yes!

Aug. [*Aside.*] Damn the Deacon! [*Aloud.*] What a scoundrel!

Jem. Complete! And the Deacon ses there's two of 'em—another scoundrel along with him, that makes b'lieve to be his servant.

Aug. Makes believe to be his servant!

Jem. Yes; and the Deacon ses all the fellers in New Canaan hev sot a watch for both of 'em, and are sure to ketch 'em and give 'em both Connecticut suits to travel off in.

Aug. A Connecticut suit!—what's that!

Jem. Tar and feathers!

Aug. No!

Jem. Yes; and the Deacon—he's a dreadful good natured crittur— he has promised to find the tar.

Aug. Oh! he finds the tar!

Jem. Yes; and old aunty Debby Higgins finds feathers. She's ripped up a feather bed on purpose.

Aug. [*Aside.*] Pleasant! [*Aloud.*] No!

Jem. Yes; and Ebenezer Sicklark ses he'll head the fellers, and ride 'em on a rail outside the town—and he'll du it. Ebenezer's tho feller that was sparkin' me afore you come: he is dreadful smart I tell yeow, and shocking powerful, and so all-fired tall he can't tell when his feet's cold; then he's proud tu, and wears shirt collars so stiff and high Sundays that he can't turn his head without cutting his ears off. But neow, I guess, he'll feel kind o' streaked and won't be so stuck up when he finds I hev gin him the sack, for of course I can't allow him tu be follerin' me round, and settin' up o' nights neow, as you are here. You wouldn't allow it, would you!

Aug. [*Aside.*] Is this simplicity, or does she know me! [*Aloud.*] Certainly not.

Jem. [*Rises.*] Wal, neow, you see that's the heow we Connecticut folks begin our sparkin'. The gals first make it interestin' to the fellers, as I hev to you; then by'm-by comes the fellows' turn, and then both become interestin' together, and that's the best part on't.

Aug. [*Aside.*] Oh, she's a downright simpleton—it's all right!

Jem. Neow come [*crosses to* R.], I want to show you tu the folks that's come tu see father's churn. We're going tu hev a time there I tell you, and if you mind—but I'll give you a chance tu do a heap of courting, and may be a leetle ——

Aug. What!

Jem. Kissing.   [*Exit,* R. H.

Aug. Oh, she's a fool!   [*Exit,* R.

SCENE VI.—*The Kitchen,* D. F. *The Churn, centre up stage over open trap.* CÆSAR *discovered locking the kitchen door. Has lighted candle.*

Cæsar. Dar, you is locked fast. I don't 'zactly know de meanin' of dis, but our Jemimy say dar is two dam rascal in dis house, and doors must be lock—de street door am lock—and now dis door am lock; and now I muss get de milk ready for show de folks how massa's churn make de butter widout turning no handle. Golly, dat churn am de churn for make de butter.

[*Goes out, talking,* U. E. R. H., *with candle, dark.*

Enter TWITCHER, *cautiously* L. H.

Twitcher. The street door locked, and the key gone. As well as I remember, this is the way I came in at the kitchen door. Confound it, where is the door. [*feels along and finds it.*] Fast locked, and no doubt the house surrounded by the gentlemen that anticipate the pleasure of fitting us on with our new suits. What is to be done! No cupboard, no dresser, no cellar door. Hark! people come this way—many feet—

[*Listens,* L. H., *and goes,* R. H.; CÆSAR *laughs outside.*

Caesar. (R.H.) Golly, massa, you don't say.

Twitcher. And others coming this way. Where shall I hide. [*Feels the churn.*] What's this, a barrel! Yes, and empty; it may afford me concealment 'till I have an opportunity of creeping out unseen, should the door be unlocked. [*Sneezes as he gets in.*] Damn this cold.

Enter CÆSAR *and* UNCLE, R. H. U. E.—CÆSAR, *with two lights; places them on table. Light Stage.*

Caesar. Golly! massa, what a passion de old missus was in when she come back.

Uncle. Yes; but I have pacified her. What Jemimy is doing is all meant for her good.

Caesar. Yes, massa; but it am dam hard for make de ole woman believe a young feller makin' lub to dem aint for dem good.

Uncle. Yes! but seeing is believing, and she will soon see, with her own eyes, that young fellow making love to another, and know him for an impostor.

Caesar. De Deacon ses dar am two ob dem 'posters—de honorable Disgustin Gash, and—[TWITCHER *sneezes.*]—what am dat!

Uncle. The cat after the milk, perhaps. But I must tell our Jemimy all is ready for her. [*Exit,* L. H.

[CAESAR *lays his finger on his nose, and creeps silently to churn—peeps in—then creeps back.*

Caesar. [*Whispers aside.*] De oder 'poster hidin'—[*points.*] Golly! [*Knock,* D. F., *goes to door.*] Who am dar!

Deacon. It's I—Deacon Peek. Open the door.

[TWITCHER *pops up his head.*

Caesar. [*Back to churn—opens door.*] What am de matter now!

[DEACON *at door, only looking in.*] Tell our Jemimy I am all ready for her here, outside.

Caesar. What am dar outside!

Deacon. She knows, those she expects, you tell her. I'll keep 'em 'till called in. [*Exit,* D. F.

Twitcher. Ebenezer and his party. O, lord! [*Pops down.*

Caesar. I wonder who dem is! [*Loud laughing,* L. H.] Golly! here all de folks come for christen de churn.

[*Looks off,* L. H. TWITCHER *looks out.*

Twitcher. [*Aside, looking at churn.*] The churn! Damme, I'm in the churn. [*Pops down.*

Enter OUR JEMIMY, AUGUSTUS *and* UNCLE, L. H.—GUESTS, *two and two, dancing in, and laughing,* D. F.

Jem. There, now, gals and fellows, you know all about my new beau, and I guess you all think him some pumpkins; but though I shall be riz considerable in the scale of human society, as the Deacon ses, when I'm married to a real, right down honorable, and one that is to be a Lord——

All. A Lord!

Jem. Yes—the Lord knows who!

Caesar. Golly!

Jem. Still I won't be proud. And if any of you should come to London, where we shall live, shan't we, spouse, that is tu be!

Aug. When we are in town.

Jem. Wal, I guess, when you marry, we will be in town! Yes, I'll welcome you the same as usual. But now, I mustn't allow future greatness tu put out of my head our present meetin', which is tu show you heou father's patent churn works. Father, you explain tu spouse, that is to be, heou the works of your churn are like a clock all inside. [UNCLE *takes* AUGUSTUS *one side,* L. H., *and seems to explain.*

Jem. [*To* CAESAR, *aside.*] Has the Deacon been here!

Caesar. Yes; he am ready wid dem, you know, at de door, and say, our Jemimy, de odder 'poster am in de churn. [*Whispers.*

Jem. What! Ha! ha! ha! Don't let on. Hush!

Uncle. [*To* AUGUSTUS.] Great improvement, isn't it. You'll see something you don't expect.

Aug. Wonderful! I'm anxious to see it tried.

Jem. Not yet. We're going tu hav a dance—then a game of blindman's buff. Father, lend me a handkerchief. [*He gives one.*] Neou blindman's buff.

All. Blindman's buff.

Jem. [*Aside to* UNCLE.] Hev aunty ready. [*To* AUGUSTUS.] Neou then, let me blind you. [*Tying on handkerchief.*] Wives that is tu be, sometimes du blind their spouses, that is to be, before marriage. He! he! he!

Aug. Yes, and sometimes husbands blind their wives after marriage. Ha! ha! ha!

Jem. [*Binding his eyes.*] I shouldn't wonder; [*Aside.*] but I guess you'll see yours has both her eyes open the first time you look at her. [*Finishing binding him.*] There. How many horses has your father got in his stable?

Aug. Perhaps fifty.

Jem. Yes, you must say; three—black, white and grey.

Aug. Three! Black, white and grey.

Jem. Turn round three times, and catch who you may.

[*Music.—She turns him round—they play—he feels about—*JEMIMA *motions* UNCLE—*he brings on* AUNTY, R. H. U. E.—OUR JEMIMY *takes her hand, passes her towards* AUGUSTUS, *he catches her—*JEMIMY *motions* AUNTY *silence—*UNCLE *seems to explain to* GUESTS *at back.*]

Jem. [*In low tones to* AUGUSTUS, AUNTY *being between her and him.*] Do you know me?

Aug. If I were blind, indeed, I would swear to my own Jemima. True love is always blind.

Jem. True love. Heou do I know you really do love me? Maybe what you said about the mistake with Aunt Jemimy, warnt no mistake, and you did really make love tu her.

Aug. Never! how could I possibly look on her and love her! let me take off——

Jem. No, no; don't unblind yet. I hev suthin tu say tu you I couldn't say with your eyes a'looking at me. But why couldn't you look on Miss Jemimy? she's almost as young as I be, and fully as handsome.

Aug. What, that red-haired harridan——

Aunt. Oh! [*Almost screaming—restrained by* JEMIMA.

Aug. What is the matter? why do you tremble?

Jem. A kinder stich in my side. Miss Jemimy is accounted handsome.

Aug. Miss Jemima, don't call her Miss-handsome; she's as homely as a hedgehog, and old as Satan. [AUNTY *going to scratch him—*JEMIMA *prevents her.*] And you never told her she was young and handsome, and you loved her.

Aug. Never—I'll swear it.

Jem. And you only love me.

Aug. You, and only you.

Jem. As true as you'll kiss me neou when you see me.

Aug. As true.

Jem. Then unbind your true love's eyes, and take the smack.

[*Passes behind to* L. H. *of* AUGUSTUS.

Aug. [*Takes off bandage—*AUNTY *slaps his face.*] Confusion, the old woman—[*Turns* L. H.] distraction, the young one. [*Runs to door flat— it opens, and* DEACON *enters with* MRS. BONNET *and four children. She has on a large bonnet.*] Damnation—my wife!

Caesar. Damnation am his wife—guess she am worser dan de odder ole woman.

Mrs. Bonnet. Oh! my Bonnet, my Bonnet! look upon your distracted wife and abandoned babes!

Aunty. His wife and babes!

[*All are forward of the churn—*TWITCHER *pops up his head, and is about to get out—*CAESAR *threatens him—he pops down.*

Mrs. B. His true and lawful wedded wife and four blessed babes, all born in wedlock. Oh, Bonnet, Bonnet, why did you ever leave me!

Jem. Aye; why, heou could he leave sich a wife, with sich a bonnet; but, however, he shall promise now tu stick to you, or he shall be fitted with a new suit that will stick to him. Is all ready, Deacon!

Deacon. All ready, and warranted to fit.

Jem. [*To* AUGUSTUS.] What d'ye say! will you stick to your wife in your old suit, or start fresh on another Connecticut sparking, in the new suit that my Ebenezer is ready tu fit on tu you!

Aug. I'll stick to the old suit and my——

Jem. Old wife! no doubt she's like a singed cat, a sight better than she looks, and will be a credit to her noble father-in-law, the lord Nozoo, with another Bonnet. And neou as you hev got what you come for—a wife, and Aunty has got clear of sich a husband as you, now we'll have a dance; so gals and boys, take your partners, and go it strong.

[*A general dance. At the end of the dance,* CAESAR *enters with a large pan of milk.*

Jem. Caesar, now turn in the milk, and we'll set Dad's patent churn going rite along.

[CAESAR *throws the milk into the churn, and* TWITCHER *starts up from it completely saturated; the party laugh, and the curtain falls.*

THE END.